THE VICTIM

TREVOR SOUTHERN

Published by
Eleusinian Press Ltd
www.eleusinianpress.co.uk

First Edition published 2017

Printed and bound in Great Britain
by Copytech (UK) Ltd

A catalogue record for this book
is available from The British Library

ISBN 978-1-909494-12-1

ONE

January 2009

Aisha Abbas, a morning supervisor led the new starter Paul Hirst along the aisle of the Fast Service C-store.

"I'll put you here on ready meals for the next hour. When it gets to eight you can go with someone and learn the tills," she told him.

Paul, a 17 year old college student smiled and said, "Thanks."

"Daniel," Aisha called out to a dark-haired slender young man. "Come work with Paul."

"Yeah, sure." Daniel Steele smiled.

Brian Lever the other morning supervisor appeared suddenly and curtly asked, "How are things going Aisha?"

"Fine, our new boy is eager to go," she said.

Brian nodded and stomped past Daniel like he wasn't there. Daniel had to jump aside. Brian then walked over to a cage of goods and started to offload.

"Who's he?" Paul asked Aisha.

"He's a part-time morning supervisor," she explained. "He trained a lot of us, and he's earned our respect."

Paul looked over at the stern-faced, small white-haired man. He seemed unapproachable and intimidating.

Aisha walked away to join Brian.

"So, how are you finding it?" Daniel asked Paul.

"All right. How long you been here?" Paul asked.

"Five months. It sucks, six am starts on Sunday morning." Daniel replied.

"I don't mind," Paul said

"That's good. I know I do." Daniel forced a laugh.

"So Mark hired him. I hope he is all right." Brian said loudly to Aisha. He glared challengingly at Daniel and said angrily. "I mean, you look at some of the people he has hired."

Daniel stared back and then looked away.

"Who's Mark?" Paul asked.

"He's the manager here. He's a twat; just like that prick over there with a short arse complex." Daniel smiled wryly, nodding in Brian's direction. "Did he not interview you?"

"Oh yeah, short tubby bloke with a beard, that him?"

"Yeah, and if he ever asks how you are I guarantee you the next question will be 'can you stay on today?' Also that comment Brian just made about 'look who he has hired', and the way he looked at me; that happens regularly. If Brian decides he doesn't like you, don't even try to make nice with him."

"All right mate," Daniel said, smiling with forced cheerfulness to another young man walking past.

The man, Tim returned the smile and walked on.

"A bit shy?" Paul asked.

"They use and abuse the poor bloke, but – that's this place for you," Daniel said.

"Daniel," Brian snapped abruptly.

"Yeah?" Daniel called back.

"Here. Now!" Brian ordered. Daniel walked over to him. "You put the delivery away this morning didn't you?"

"I did help to."

"So why did you put eggs out when there were older ones out there?" Brian demanded.

"Someone else brought those out. How was I to know?" Daniel asked.

Brian clenched his fists and gritted his teeth. "You should have seen them and realised."

"I don't see how." Daniel replied edgily.

"You should be aware of things. Out drinking last night were you? No consideration or respect for this place."

"This place shows me none," Daniel snapped.

"We put up with you every week even though you're stupid and slow and a waste of space. You're lucky anywhere would want you."

"Are you fucking finished?" Daniel demanded.

"No I'm not. The hours you're stuck with you may hate but that's why you're kept on. You should be grateful for the job. Better people than you are unemployed out there."

"All right, you've made your point."

"Right, now you're going to put all those eggs back and put the old ones out."

"All the bad things in this world and you -" Daniel began.

"Stop talking, right now," Brian said "I've had enough of you."

"As have I!" Daniel shouted. His right fist shot out hitting Brian just below the right eye. Brian fell back stunned and Daniel moved quickly.

He threw a second punch to Brian's gut then grabbed the stunned supervisor by the scruff of the neck and threw him hard into a fridge. Milk bottles fell and exploded on the ground and onto Daniel's trousers. Breathing heavily he stood over the dazed supervisor. "You arrogant, ignorant, insensitive CUNT!" he screamed, and spat at Brian. He then turned around and stormed out of the store.

TWO

Police Sergeant Ridgley and PC Black walked into the Fast Service C-store twenty minutes later. As it was now just after seven, the shop was now open and early morning customers were in. Shop workers continued to put things out, and two were on the tills. A short tubby man with a beard dressed in a shirt and tie came forward.

"I'm Mark Edmunds, the manager here," he said to the police officers. "Thank you for coming."

Ridgley asked "How's the man who was assaulted?"

"He's in the staff room with the paramedics. He got hit pretty hard and thrown too. I've closed off the milk section as I know you will need to examine it." Mark sighed. "I've had to put milk cages by the till and put someone by the milk fridge to keep people away. This is really causing me a headache."

Ridgley frowned and Mark led them along the aisle.

"So this Daniel Steele, what can you tell me about him?" Ridgley asked.

"A waste of space," Mark said. "I'm glad to be rid of him. But not like this."

He led them to the staff room where two paramedics stood over Brian Lever, who lay on a stretcher, with his neck in a brace in case of neck injury. Ridgley introduced himself.

"How are you?" he asked.

"My face hurts, so does my back. Have you caught him yet?"

"No," Ridgley said. "But speaking from experience I expect he will turn himself in or he'll be at his home address where we'll go after him. Do you feel up to making a brief statement, Mr Lever? I mean you don't have to, and a detective will soon interview you formally anyway."

One of the paramedics, a tall middle aged man said, "We'd like to take him to hospital to check his back out. We think it's nothing serious, but we would like to take him to be checked out."

"Of course." Ridgley smiled. To Brian he said. "Could I just take your name and address?"

Black took out a pen and notepad and wrote as Brian relayed the information.

"And the name of the man who assaulted you?" Ridgley asked.

"Daniel Steele." Brian replied.

Ridgley turned to Mark. "We'll need Daniel Steele's address, and to talk to any of your workers who saw it. Plus the CCTV footage."

"Two did: Aisha Abbas and Paul Hirst. It's that poor lad's first day. What a start." Mark shook his head. "Plus I reckon the security camera got it pretty good."

Daniel Steele lived fifteen minutes walk from the town centre. He felt dazed and stunned by what he had done, but the burning rage was still there. When he got to his house he breathed deeply and composed himself before taking out his key and walking in. He went into the kitchen. His father was still asleep, but his mother was there with a cup of tea. She looked surprised.

"What are you doing back?" she asked.

Daniel put his hands to the back of his head. "I walked out, mum. I've just had enough."

"Why, what happened?"

"That supervisor, Brian, I told you about. He upset me, so I told him where to go and walked out."

"But Daniel, if you apologise they might take you back."

"I won't apologise, that place does my head in. Sorry, Mum, I just need to be alone for a bit."

He walked to his room and lay down on his bed. Over the next five minutes thoughts came to him. They would send the police here. Brian was the type to press charges over something like this. He stood up and took his uniform tie off, put it on the bed. He walked downstairs and put his coat back on.

"I'm going for a walk," Daniel called out and left before any reply could come. He felt bad for his parents. They would get an unpleasant shock when the police arrived. He walked for ten minutes. He looked around. The street was empty. He took out his phone and dialled 999.

"999; what service do you require?" a woman's voice asked.

"Police please."

"One minute."

A male voice then came on. "Police operator. What's your emergency?"

Daniel blurted out, "My name is Daniel Steele. I assaulted a man earlier this morning. I would like to turn myself in."

"All right, Mr Steele, where are you?"

"I'm in Southlands Road, Mansford."

"Thank you.. Now can you tell me about the incident?"

"I don't remember too well. Just that we were arguing at work and I attacked him."

"Where was this, and who did you attack?" the operator asked.

"His name is Brian Lever and it was at the Fast Service store in Mansford. I'm sorry, I can't really think."

"Very well. Just tell me when."

"About half an hour ago."

"Alright. A car will be there shortly." The line went dead.

Daniel put his phone away and breathed heavily. The cold January air chilled him, but not as much as the thought that he was about to be arrested.

He had never been in trouble with the police. Now he was to be arrested for assaulting a 57-year-old man. He looked at the time: 7:47. He breathed heavily again and tried to stay with it. He fought off the thought of prison. As a karate blue belt he reckoned they would go hard on him.

Twenty minutes later a police car came around the corner. It parked and two middle aged policemen got out. The taller of the two asked sternly.

"Are you Daniel Steele?"

"Yes I am. I am coming quietly. I won't resist."

"Put your hands out please." The shorter one said, taking out the hand cuffs. Daniel complied and the shorter man cuffed him. The taller one said,

"Daniel Steele, I am arresting you for the assault on Brian Lever. You do not have to say anything now, but it may harm your defence if you fail to mention something that you later rely on in court. Anything you do say will be used as evidence in a court of law. Do you understand?"

"Yes sir." Daniel answered quietly, his earlier aggression gone, he did not move as the shorter one searched him for offensive items. He felt destroyed by the fear of being in a situation that he could not have imagined. He replied flatly as the taller officer questioned him about the assault but he could not give answers, his mind blank, the shock had kicked in.

THREE

Two hours later in the Criminal Investigation Department at Mansford police station Detective Sergeant Michael Rivers and Detective Constable Chris Walker walked into the office of Detective Inspector Elizabeth Burroughs. Her office was efficiently tidy and well-spaced as Burroughs demanded all her officers' desks to be.

"Morning ma'am." Rivers said.

"DS Rivers, DC Walker, please come in and close the door," she replied.

"I understand a man was assaulted today at a high street store." Rivers said.

"Yes," the tall, slender DI said. "This is what we have. 57-year-old Brian Lever, a semi-retired engineering director, who is now a supervisor at a Fast Service C-store was punched twice and thrown into a fridge. The offender is 24-year-old Daniel Steele who turned himself in two hours ago."

"Does he have previous?" Walker asked.

"No, the arresting officers did a PDA. He was a fellow worker who took offence to a bollocking he was getting and assaulted Mr Lever. We have Steele in custody and the hospital says Mr Lever is up for making a statement. I need you two to go there and take it and then charge Daniel Steele."

"Will Lever press charges ma'am?" Rivers asked.

"I think he would like to, yes."

Fifteen minutes later they walked into the hospital.

"What do you think?" Walker asked Rivers. "Open and shut case?"

"I'd say so, but, it's a case of how bad the injuries are and what sort of a person Daniel Steele is," Rivers replied. He took out his warrant card as he got to the reception desk. "Good morning. We are DS Rivers and DC Walker. We're here to interview Brian Lever. Could you tell us where he is please?" Rivers said showing his warrant card.

The receptionist directed them, Rivers thanked her and they went to see him. The nurse at the ward desk led them to Brian. Rivers smiled and showed his ID.

"Hello, Mr Lever. I'm DS Michael Rivers, this is DC Chris Walker. How are you?"

"My face has swelled up, my stomach is sore and my back's got external and internal bruising from what that little thug did. Have you caught him yet?"

Rivers nodded at him. "Yes, he turned himself in, but we decided to come and see you first before we speak to him, as he currently refuses to speak. And your injuries have been photographed."

"I'd say it's bloody obvious what's happened."

"Yes, but we need details of what led up to it, and what you know of Daniel Steele."

"He's a waste of space. After five months he still can't find where a lot of things go. Always ready with an attitude too. Continually complains about having to do early shifts on Saturdays and Sundays. He only whinged to me once, mind. I just told him if he didn't like it he should quit."

"What is he likely to say about you?" Rivers asked.

"No doubt he will claim I victimised him and gave him a hard time. If his ethic improved it'd be different. I'm hard but fair. Oh, and also he constantly came in weekend mornings still drunk from the previous night. He'd go out till two in the morning and then come in four hours later. I'll tell you this though – watch him – he's a charmer! He knows how to get people on his side; not to mention he has some very dodgy friends. You might want to make sure he won't use them to intimidate me."

After they had his statement the two walked back to Rivers' car.

"What do you think?" Walker asked. "Seems to me we've got a dedicated hard worker assaulted by a slack employee who kicked off for being held to account."

"Maybe, but I'd like to speak to Steele first before drawing any conclusions about it."

FOUR

Daniel sat on the flat bed of his cell staring at the walls around him and the locked door. He had done several repetitions of push-ups on the bed to keep his mind occupied, but, now the depression of being here had got to him. He had used his phone call to call home. His mother had cried and his father had sounded angry, but sad. Then he had met Robert Woods, the duty solicitor, who had advised him to stay silent until charged. So he had. His phone, wallet shoes and keys were all in police custody. He stared at his empty meal pack and the cup of water that he had had. Waiting. Waiting to be charged with assault.

The cell flap opened and a male face peered in to look at him and then the cell door opened and a PC that looked younger than him stood there.

"Come on. Time to go."

Daniel nodded. The PC stepped aside and told Daniel to walk in front of him and directed him to an interview room. His solicitor sat inside with two men dressed in suits: One blonde, the other dark-haired. Daniel sat next to his solicitor. The dark-haired man turned on the tape recorder, then spoke.

"All right interview commencing 11.09 am. Present are DS Rivers and..."

"DC Walker," Walker said.

Daniel remembered Woods telling him that they stated their names individually for the benefit of the tape.

Rivers continued, "We're here with the accused, Daniel Steele and his solicitor."

"Robert Woods." Woods said.

Rivers looked at Daniel. "Daniel my name is Detective Sergeant Michael Rivers; do you understand why you are here?"

"Yes." Daniel replied.

"Very well." Rivers leant back. "Daniel Steele, you have been charged with the actual bodily harm of Brian Lever. You've made a confession. Do you wish to say anything further?"

Daniel put his head in his hands and then looked at Rivers and Walker; their faces stern and unsympathetic.

"Do you realise the seriousness of what you have done?" Rivers asked. "You attacked a man who is more than thirty years older than you."

Daniel looked at him. "How is he?"

"Do you really care?"

"Yeah, because it affects my chances of getting off."

"Give me a good reason why you should get off."

"What's the point? You two have pre-judged me anyway."

I see what Brian meant by the attitude, Rivers thought.

"Sorry, but may I speak?" Woods asked.

"Of course." Rivers told him.

Woods faced Daniel. "What you said to me earlier. Tell them."

"You think they'll care? I'm condemned in their eyes."

"Try it." Woods smiled.

"Daniel, why shouldn't we think you guilty?" Walker asked. "I mean, you admit to what you did. You were witnessed assaulting him. What defence could you have?"

"What did you tell your solicitor?" Rivers pressed.

"That Brian Lever is a bully. All he ever does is get on my case."

"Do you think that made it right to thump him?" Rivers asked.

"No. But he might think before upsetting people like that again, bastard."

"There's more," Woods said.

"All right. Talk to Stacey Willis and Adam Chester. This isn't so black and white," Daniel said.

"We also understand you have friends who might try and intimidate Brian Lever." Rivers said

"Oh come off it. They wouldn't do that."

"You should hope they don't."

"Am I likely to get bail?"

"It's up to the magistrate on this occasion." Rivers explained. "Not me. In two days, I reckon, you'll have a bail hearing. You'll have to prove you have no intent of running off. The magistrate will also consider the severity of the assault. If you are granted bail there will be conditions attached. If not you will be held in secure accommodation until the trial. Anything else?"

"No."

"Good. We'll need you to make a statement. Your lawyer will be present and a family member or someone close to you as well if you want, is that understood?" Rivers told him.

"Yes, thanks."

"Right, interview terminated at 11.14 am."

Daniel was taken back to his cell. Rivers stood with Walker and Woods.

"I want to know what kind of defence he wants to mount." Walker said.

"Now you know I can't say," Woods said.

"But what possible defence could he have?" Walker persisted.

"No comment." Woods smiled wryly and walked away.

Later, DI Burroughs wanted the detectives to brief her.

"What did you make of Steele?" she asked.

Rivers replied, "A tough one to crack, ma'am. He's cagey. His solicitor will hopefully get him to open up. He also hinted at a not guilty plea."

"What?"

"Yeah, we think there's something being held back. I think they're planning on making Lever out to be a bully who pushed Steele over the edge."

"Anything else?"

"Yeah, Lever mentioned Steele has some 'dodgy' friends. I want to find out who they are and make sure they know we'll be watching them." Rivers said.

"How do you propose to do that?" DI Burroughs asked.

"We need to speak with all at Fast Service anyway. Hopefully I'll find out a hangout for Steele's friends and go there looking for character witnesses, and that way find out who they are."

FIVE

Mark Edmunds leaned back as he listened to Rivers on the phone.

"Yeah," he said. "Your guys have let me have my milk section back. I called the hospital a short while ago and they said Brian will need two to four weeks rest. Understandable. I'm just glad you got Daniel Steele locked up, little bastard. Being difficult is he? That makes a change. Yes, of course you can talk to people here. Just let me know when. I can provide a fair few people who will speak for Brian. Oh, really?... Well, yes, if he said to speak to them, then so you should. I can arrange a time. Just let me know when... All right, cheers. Bye now." He hung up.

It was no surprise to him to hear that Daniel wanted to imply bullying. And he thought Daniel was being devious to name two people to the police who would back that up. Well, Mark couldn't stop them talking to the police, but he could make sure Stacey and Adam knew the consequences of being disloyal to the management. He walked onto the shop floor. Both were on tills.

Both were in their early twenties, shy and lacked confidence to question or do much. Neither of them had much ambition in life.

"Adam, Stacey? Can I speak to you after you've got this queue down?" he said.

He walked back. A few minutes later they came in.

"Close the door." Mark said, facing them in his chair. They stood before him nervously. "Now as you're aware Daniel has been charged with the assault on Brian this morning. The police want to speak with us about him and Brian. And all being fair he's asked for you to speak for him."

"I'd be happy to." Adam said.

"Yeah, and me," Stacey added.

"Well, that's fine. You can talk about the better side of him; tell the police that he was OK to you. But – I don't want you speaking ill about Brian to them. Understood?"

Adam had a bit more confidence then Stacey. "But why?"

"What Daniel did was wrong. Do we have any dispute about that?" Mark asked.

They shook their heads. "I have to consider what's good for this store, and let me be blunt: things are the way they are because they have to be. You may not like how Brian does some things, I know I don't. But I do not want you two or anyone else bad-mouthing either me or him or anything else to the police. Running a convenience store is demanding and so I must say to anyone who complains about how things are – put up or fuck off."

His voice had lost its easy charm and was now threatening. "I will be checking the statements that you make."

He doubted he could do that, but they were too dim to know or question that. "If I find you've said anything bad about Brian or me or the way things are here then I will see to it that you are dismissed."

Mark looked at their nervous faces and thought how weak and pathetic they were. "And given how neither of you are great assets here it's safe to assume that you'd struggle to get decent employment anywhere else. So as your way of thanking me for putting up with you and Brian for his tolerance, you will not say anything bad about us. Is that clear?"

"So what should we say about Brian?" Stacey whispered.

"Just that you work with him and he's got his way of doing things. He may be tough, but he's efficient. And he is. Now there are a lot of customers out there, so get back out there and serve them."

Mark watched them go. Put up or fuck off was how he did things. Most people working here either found it convenient to them, or they had nothing else to go for.

SIX

The Silver Seal pub was as busy as it usually was on a Sunday afternoon: people were getting together on their day off or just for their lunch breaks. It was a place that catered to a large amount of locals and to university and college students. It was a very old pub, built in the early nineteenth century, and despite a lot of more modern updates, a lot of the old architecture still remained.

Two men stood at the bar, one tall and strongly built, in his mid-forties with short brown hair, sipping a pint of lager. The other was younger, in his late twenties, the same height, but fatter and in poor physical shape.

"You heard about Daniel?" the older man asked.

"No. Is he all right?"

"He's been arrested."

"Daniel? I don't believe it. Who told you?"

"I nipped in to his shop on the way to work this morning," the older man said. "I just did a couple of hours on site; asked after him and was told he'd been nicked for attacking someone else there."

"It finally came out. I always said to Daniel he should stick up for himself more -"

The older man glared at his friend. "Joe, shut up right now. Until now Daniel had the sense to keep his cool and not run his mouth off like you."

"I'm just saying that he let things build up, Pete. That's all."

Pete, the older man just stared grimly ahead.

"So what happened to you then? Get mugged?" The old man in the neighbouring bed asked Brian Lever.

"No; a work dispute. This young idiot lost his temper because I was telling him off about something and attacked me." Brian replied.

"They're too soft these days these young pups. Can't take it, can they?"

"No, but in this day and age with all this political correctness it's hard to do your job. As a supervisor, I consider myself hard and demanding, but fair. All I ask is that people do what they're supposed to, and in the store I work at, there are those that do. Sadly there are those that are a waste of time and who there really is no hope for."

Daniel had slept badly, and the duty officer waking him several times that night to check on him had not helped. When he finally was woken he was given breakfast. Once he had eaten the cell door opened again. The young PC and Woods stood at his cell door.

"Good morning Daniel. How did you sleep?" Woods asked.

"Not well. It's not home." Daniel managed a smile.

"OK then, you're going to be driven to court."

Daniel was hand cuffed and led into a security van. Two other men, both older and both violent looking sat in the back with him. A brawny security guard sat with them. No words were spoken. Daniel just stared at the floor. It had sunk in what was happening, but while the anger in him had faded, the shock was still there. He thought of having to face his family and friends. He had an older brother and a younger sister. They were both in high-end jobs and doing well, and who was he? A man who drifted from job to job and was now on trial for assault. Unless the Crown Prosecution Service dropped the charges which was unlikely.

When they arrived at the courts they were taken in the back way and handed over to security. Security took them to a waiting room where they sat down.

"Hey," one of the other men said to Daniel. "What 'ave you been accused of?"

"Assault on my supervisor." Daniel replied.

The man grinned showing a couple of broken teeth. "I'm sure the cunt deserved it."

"How about you?" Daniel asked.

"Nutted my missus' bit on the side a few times. Little snitch can't take it and grassed me up."

Daniel looked at the security guards nearby. "You want to be saying that in front of them?"

"Bollocks to them." The man grinned. "I'm done for anyway. I don't give a shit."

One of the security guards' radios went off. He answered it.

"Right thanks," he said. He looked at the man. "Jamie Mayne, time to go. Play nice now ok?"

"Yeah." The man, Mayne got up and walked to the guards. "Good luck mate," he said to Daniel.

"Thanks," Daniel replied. He watched two guards lead Mayne away.

A few minutes later the radio went off again. The lead guard stepped forward.

"Daniel Steele?"

"Yeah?"

"All right Steele, they're ready for you, son. Let's go."

Daniel was lead into a court room. He looked around. The district judge, an elderly man, wasn't even looking at him. He saw Woods who looked over and smiled at him. Daniel sat on a plastic chair. The clerk, a young woman then stood up. Daniel felt himself pulled up by a guard. Irritated, he shrugged the man off.

"You are Daniel Oliver Steele?" the clerk asked.

"Yes."

"Thank you Mr Steele, you may sit," the clerk said.

Daniel smiled and complied.

"Mr Steele," the district judge said. "You are charged with assault on a Mr Brian Lever. Mr Woods?"

"Yes, your honour." Woods rose.

"Does your client understand what he has been charged with?"

"Yes, he does."

"Very well. This is just a bail hearing. Mr Woods, if you would be good enough to outline your request for bail."

Woods spoke of how his client was of good previous character, with many friends and family in the local area, and of no threat of a flight risk, or to the victim. At the end the judge spoke.

"I find no reason therefore to deny bail. Unless Mr Brand you wish to object?"

Daniel breathed a sigh of relief. Brand, a slender blonde haired man stood.

"Your honour, if I may. I will not oppose bail. However I will ask for conditions to apply."

"Yes, of course. I was going to set them. Please tell me if you have any additional ones to my own. Please stand, Mr Steele."

"Yes, sir." Daniel said as he stood.

"Mr Steele, bail is granted, but will be revoked if you breach any of the following conditions. Firstly you are banned from approaching Brian Lever and the Fast Service store. Secondly you are to sign in every Tuesday at the local police station. Lastly you are not to approach any of your former colleagues to try and influence their opinions. Do you accept these terms?"

"Yes sir."

"Good. Mr Brand, anything else?"

"Yes your honour. I would like to request Mr Steele does not discuss this with his friends."

Woods looked stunned at Brand while the judge merely smiled.

"I feel that unfair, Mr Brand. This will be in the local paper and it will be difficult for Mr Steele not to talk about it."

"Very well. That is all." Brand sat down.

"Right, court is adjourned." The judge said.

A guard came forward and undid Daniel's hand cuffs. Daniel was lead out and taken out to the waiting room where he was met by the man he recognised as DC Walker.

Walker looked at him. "Well done on making bail, Daniel."

"Thanks, what's up?"

"I've heard you have some… er… interesting mates. Mates who I fear may try and persuade Brian Lever to drop the charges."

Daniel swallowed hard. "They probably will want to, but I can sincerely assure you I'll tell them not to get involved."

"And I'm to trust that? Who are they?"

"I can't say."

"I could revoke your bail. Say you do pose a threat."

Woods seemed to appear out of nowhere and cut in: "If I may point out DC Walker, whoever these friends are more likely to go after Brian Lever if Daniel's inside than if he's out."

Walker shook his head. "I'll be seeing you both." He walked off.

"Thanks." Daniel said.

"He's lucky I don't make a complaint for making a threat." Woods said quietly. "Listen, Daniel. If we're to go for a not guilty plea I need to make you out to be the victim of harassment and unfair treatment that led to you being pushed to the point where you did not see any wrong in what you did. To give you the brief version."

"Do you really think the police care?"

"To be blunt, no. But what goes on your statement goes before the judge and the jury. That's what counts. I need you to be more open in the interviews. I've dealt with Walker and Rivers before and I find Walker only sees things in black and white, but Rivers is more open minded. While you can't have Rivers on your side I think you can get him to empathise a bit."

"What will that do?"

Woods grinned. "Make it hard for him. Look I've defended some right bastards in my time, but, I really want to help you because I think you are a decent person who got pushed over the edge, and while I can't justify assault I think we can limit the damage."

Daniel walked out, in some ways feeling like a free man. His parents waited for him at the court entrance. His mother hugged him. Daniel stepped back and smiled.

"I'm all right."

"We're not," his father said. "What were you thinking?"

"I'm sorry, dad. That place finally pushed me over the edge."

Mr Steele touched his shoulder. "All right, Dan. Let's get you home. I'm just glad they let you walk."

SEVEN

Early Tuesday afternoon Daniel held a copy of the Midweek Chronicle. His home town Mansford's local paper in his hands. His story had made page 5.

ASSAULT IN LOCAL C-STORE

A semi-retired man was assaulted at a local Fast Service store on Sunday morning.

Brian Lever, 57, a part-time supervisor was allegedly attacked by a co-worker during an argument.

A 24-year-old local man has been arrested and charged with ABH, but was remanded on bail.

Police are continuing to investigate.

A minute later his phone rang.

"All right, Joe."

"Yeah, how are you feeling?"

"Like I've got a prison sentence over my head."

"Pete doubts it, and he knows where he's coming from. Do you want to meet us at the Seal now?"

"All right, see you in a bit."

Later Daniel stood with Joe McGinty, Pete Redmond, Evan Pearson and Rees Carlton. Evan and Rees were both in their mid-thirties.

"All right son, heard about your grief. That supervisor was it?" Pete asked.

"Yeah, I just lost it, you know? I'm not paid to be dealing with that. Well, at least I don't have to worry about early morning starts at the weekend and late nights in the week."

"What a little snitch." Joe growled. "Picks on people, and then throws a hissy fit when he gets what's coming to him."

"It's his prerogative, but I wouldn't worry about it Daniel. You're not looking at much time in prison, if any." Pete told him. "And I should know."

"Well, for now I'll try and relax. I got loads of money saved, so I'll try and enjoy myself." Daniel said.

Watching them from the Seal's other bar opposite them was a tall strongly built man wearing jeans and a light green collared shirt. He waved the girl serving drinks over.

"Can I speak to your manager?" he asked.

"Yeah, everything all right?"

"Fine and dandy. Can I speak to him?"

She nodded and walked off. She returned with a young short man.

"Hi. How can I help?" He smiled.

"I'd like to speak aside," the man said and they walked away.

The man dug something out of his pocket. "DC Craig Spears. I'm guessing you know what one of your regulars here, Daniel Steele did on Sunday?"

"Yeah, but he's behaving."

"It's not his behaviour that concerns me. I need to know the names of his mates over there."

The manager looked nervous. "They won't like me doing that."

"They won't know Mr – uh?"

"Shane Smith."

"Right, Mr Smith. I'll be honest with you. We are a bit concerned some of them may try to intimidate the victim. If anything did happen it would come back on you for being un-cooperative."

Shane sighed and rattled the names off of the men Daniel was standing with. Spears took the names down.

"Right, are there any other people I should know about?"

"There are three more regular friends of his. A guy called Ricky. I don't know his last name, but he's a shy type. Alan Saunders and Matt Tyrell, but Matt's a computer analyst or something. Can't imagine he'd be dangerous."

"Right, thanks. I'll see you." Spears exited.

"What do you think? Pay the cunt a visit when he's back at work? Let him know who he is dealing with." Joe said angrily.

"I'm for it." Pete said grimly.

"Guys," Shane cut in. "Be careful what you say. I just had a cop sniffing around asking about you lot."

"What did you tell him?" Joe demanded.

Shane sighed. He decided to be honest. "He wanted your names, so I told him. He said it would go bad for me if I didn't co-operate."

"You stupid twat, he was having you on!" Joe snarled, stepping towards the bar.

"It doesn't -" Daniel started.

Pete grabbed Joe by the shirt and pulled him over.

"That may be right Joe. Shane, nothing would have come back on you. But it doesn't make any fucking difference. So he knows who we are?"

"They'd find out one way or the other." Evan chipped in.

"We can't go for the so-called victim now." Joe argued.

"I don't want you to anyway." Daniel said. "Brian Lever is too stubborn. He'd never drop the charges."

Back at the station Spears handed the list over.

"Thanks," Rivers smiled, "I owe you one. Check them all for records Chris." He told Walker. Walker nodded and dutifully took the list.

"What do you make of Steele?" Spears asked.

"I don't know. Mark Edmunds provided us with five people who gave statements saying he was verbally aggressive at times. Rude to customers, slow to pick things up, always bad mouthing this, that and the other and slack. All spoke highly of Brian Lever."

"So a bastard with attitude who just lost his rag." Spears grinned.

"I wonder if there's more to it than that." DC Sandra Cole cut in. Rivers stared at her. "Don't you find it odd Edmunds provided you character witnesses, rather than letting you pick them out? Did anyone speak for Steele?"

"Yes, the two he recommended. Said he was all right with them; said he did put in graft, but confirmed his verbal rants about how unfair his shifts were. Neither spoke badly of Lever. Ironic he was an engineer with a name like that." Rivers replied.

"Right, verbal rants, slow to pick things up. Sounds like a person with issues to me." Cole said.

"All right, Sandra, don't start that therapist shit of yours." Spears said irritably.

"No, let her." Rivers said.

"Slow learner, slack, attitude, verbal rants. These are three signs of a frustrated person with problems," Cole said.

"Or just can't be arsed to work." Walker chuckled as he jotted more notes down. "Sarge, are you going to love what I'm finding out about his friends."

"So what do you suggest?" Rivers asked Cole.

"Speak to his parents. Find reliable close friends and talk to them," Cole said.

"Do me a favour, Sandra." Walker smirked. "Lever's the victim here, not Steele."

"Well, I need a statement from Steele still. I'll press his solicitor for it. By the way, CPS has moved in another prosecutor, George Hague. Anyone know him?"

"Yeah, he's a tosser." Spears said. "When I was investigating a robbery at a store, we had two guys in the dock. He interrogated me like I was the defendant. Woods has no chance against him."

"For a young duty solicitor Woods is efficient." Rivers said.

"Right." Walker spun around grinning. "Four of the seven named do have previous. Pete Redmond, an ex-army combat specialist. Did five of eight years inside for GBH. Rees Carlton; three years for armed robbery. Evan Pearson, one caution for breaking a bloke's jaw."

"Just a caution!" Spears was stunned.

"Yeah, the other guy attacked him. This bloke was a known street yob who would have done the same. So as you can imagine not much sympathy. Oh, yeah, Alan Saunders doesn't have a record – yet. He's awaiting trial for his part in a brawl late last year."

"Talk about the Addams family of friends." Rivers said. "Right, I'll pay Steele a visit, let him know that we know who his friends are."

In the Silver Seal a group of teenage girls were out celebrating a birthday. A man in his late forties stood at the bar. As one girl walked past he reached out and pinched her left breast and then her bottom.

"How rude!" she exclaimed and walked on.

Evan, a father of a teenage daughter had seen it though and a look of pure rage came over him. He charged over to the man.

"You think it's all right to do that, do you?" Evan threw him back and then Joe and Rees grabbed him and pulled him back. "Get off me. I can't allow that!"

"Watch it. You want police here with Daniel about?" Rees demanded.

"I think he's going to call them," Joe looked over at the man who had his phone out.

"Go on then!" Daniel snapped. "You can explain why he went for you!"

By then, Pete was over. He put restraining hands on Evan's shoulders.

"We don't need the police here. For Daniel's sake. They're looking for any excuse to take away his bail." He turned to the man who still stood with his phone in his hand. "Your kind aren't welcome here. Fuck off."

"Why don't you make me?" the man snapped.

Pete gritted his teeth. "You just groped a teenage girl. I just have to repeat it to a few people and you get lynched. Now fuck off."

"They asked for it; dressed like that." The man sighed and left the pub.

"Next time I see you I'll put you in hospital, you prick!" Evan yelled.

"Just leave it," Pete said calmly.

EIGHT

Mike Rivers drove to the Steele house alone. Walker had asked him to come but he'd declined. He would prefer to sort this out alone. He had asked Walker to update Burroughs, saying how they believed there was a strong risk of witness intimidation. Rivers arrived and got out. It was a nice house, reasonably big with a well-tended garden. He went to the house and rang the doorbell. Mrs Steele, a thin, brown-haired, middle aged woman came to the front door.

"Detective Sergeant Mike Rivers," he said, showing his warrant card. "I'm sorry to bother you. Is Daniel home?"

"No, he left for the gym a little while ago."

"OK, may I speak with you for a bit?"

"Yes, come in."

Rivers followed her to the living room where he sat down. Mrs Steele looked at him.

"I'm glad to have this chance to talk to you about Daniel. You can say I'm biased as his mother, but Daniel is a good sort. It's only over the last two years that he's started to lose it a bit."

"What do you mean?"

"Daniel was the victim of a knife attack when he was nineteen. These street thugs held him, taunted him and slashed him up."

"I see."

"He tried to carry on with his life, but, things got on top of him. He worked at the local supermarket for three years. Seemed happy most of the time, but then he just left. He told me he needed a change, but, I sense there was more.

"He went to work in the local hardware store, that small one in Holmer Road. They sacked him after only three months, claiming he wasn't showing enough initiative, but I think the real reason was his problems."

"What sort of problems?"

"He's dyspraxic. I found out recently from a friend in the supermarket that some idiots there called it 'dyspastica'."

"Did he go to the Fast Service store straight after?"

"No, he started learning through 'Train to Gain'. He went into therapy as he had planned, but all of a sudden he went to work at the Fast Service store."

She sighed. "The shifts they gave him meant he had to stop therapy. He could only go to karate, which he loved, every two or three weeks."

"What shifts was he expected to do?"

"He had to do six am till two every Saturday and Sunday. Then three pm till eleven at night, three weekdays which kept changing. I gather the manager there was not very sympathetic to his problems. What will happen to Daniel?"

Rivers smiled. "I'm afraid I can't say. Thanks for your help. I think I see now what Daniel was reluctant to tell us."

Walker and Spears stood before Burroughs.

"Ma'am, DC Spears found out the people we have to watch. Several have records and we do fear they will attempt to intimidate Brian Lever." Walker explained.

"I see. Who are they?" she asked. Walker held the printouts forward. "Pete Redmond did five years of eight for GBH twenty years ago. Rees Carlton did three of five for armed robbery several years ago. Evan Pearson, first and only caution for assault. Alan Saunders, awaiting trial for a street brawl in November last year. Redmond was also charged twice with assault last year, but in both cases the charges got dropped."

"Then again both cases were some bloke starting on him, and then crying about losing. No real sympathy for 'em," Spears said.

"Assault is a crime, DC Spears; we have a term called 'reasonable force'." Burroughs snapped.

Walker's phone rang. He answered it "Sarge? OK. Sure, Yeah... What was that?... All right then." He hung up. "DS Rivers wants me to let Steele know we know about his friends. He's at the leisure centre gym now."

"Fine, Spears go with him." Burroughs ordered.

"Ma'am?" Spears said.

"We have to assume Daniel Steele is dangerous, as he's flown off the handle once, he could do so again," she explained.

Mansford Leisure Centre's gym had two floors. Downstairs was the main weights room. Daniel was enjoying being on his own in the free weights room, away from the busy main floor with the treadmills and screens and bustle. He was using the Freedom Trainer to do bicep curls when he heard.

"Daniel Steele."

He looked over and saw Walker and a big built man walk down the stairs. They stood in front of him.

"Can I help?" Daniel asked.

"This is DC Spears," Walker said.

"You looked good on that, Daniel," Spears said. "Training to punch out another old man are we?"

"No, to keep myself occupied. Getting another job will be hard," Daniel said.

"I can imagine." Walker said. "Still it's your own fault. We took statements from your former colleagues. They say you're a bit of a head case. They also say Brian Lever's a good guy."

"Oh, let me guess. Mark Edmunds gave you the people to interview?"

"What pissed you off about Lever so much?" Spears asked. "Did you see a man who had been successful in life, and was good at his job? It reminded you of what a failure you are, so you lashed out."

"No. He was a bullying bastard, if you talked to other -"

"Lazy, useless types like you Daniel?" Walker cut in.

"Listen, he had a successful career behind him. Yes, he was good at his job, yes. But did he have any friends? No. The only true wealth a person can have is friends," Daniel snapped. "And you have to wonder why he had no friends; none that I know of anyway."

"Yes, that's why we came," Walker said. "We know who your mates are, Daniel. We know their background."

"It's in the past. They're all honest, hard-working types now."

"That makes it all right then does it?" Walker demanded.

"No way. They don't deny it either. Why don't you chase those petty thugs who like to do people over for fun."

"Like you did to Brian Lever?" Spears snarled. "Listen, we think you'll try and intimidate him and the witnesses with your thug army. We're here to let you know we'll be watching you lot." His voice became a whisper and Daniel suddenly wished other people were around. "Someone like you loses it because they're unhappy with how their life is and so they take it out on someone. A decent type who reminds them of what a failure they are." Spears stared Daniel down.

"We're done here," Walker said. The two detectives turned and went up the stairs, leaving Daniel seething.

"Ignorant bastards," he muttered.

NINE

Rivers had first gone to the local supermarket where, flashing his warrant card, he had many people say what a nice guy Daniel was – how he just got more upset than most people over things. One young man with blonde hair on the meat and fish counter had sniggered and said Daniel was always saying about people having a problem with him. He couldn't realise he was just little Daniel to them."

"What about the taunts about his learning difficulties?" Rivers had asked.

"Try working with someone like that. He was a pain in the arse. A bit simple I think."

"Did he work hard?"

"Yeah, but you had to explain everything ten times to him. Hey, Sean," he'd then called out.

A tall slender man in a section manager uniform walked over.

"The detective is here about Daniel assaulting someone," the blonde man said.

Sean laughed, "There's nothing of Daniel Steele. He's a little bloke who is a bit simple and shouldn't be starting on anyone."

"It's comments like that that cause a lot of trouble, sir," Rivers said sternly. "It's my understanding he was getting called 'dyspastic' by people here."

"Oh, it was just a bit of fun and banter. Only a few of us did it." Sean grinned.

Rivers bit down on the comment that came to mind. "You are?"

"Sean Mortimer. You're not doing an investigation into me are you?" he laughed.

"Relax, I'm not."

On his next visit to the Fast Service store Rivers asked to speak to Edmunds.

"Is this necessary? I'm very busy," Edmunds had bristled.

"It will only take a little time," Rivers had assured him. In the office he then asked, "Is it true Daniel Steele is dyspraxic?"

"What's that got to do with anything?"

"Is it true?"

"So he said... Means nothing to me. It's not exactly rocket science putting stuff out and swiping things through a till."

"Does it not explain why he had trouble learning where things were?"

"You're entitled to your opinion. I don't think so. I think he's just lazy."

"Did Brian Lever give him a hard time over it?"

"Yeah, he did. But only 'cos Daniel tried his patience. I know one time he lobbed an empty box at him out of pure frustration."

"Mmm, secondly, is it true Steele was meant to be in therapy?"

"I told him only if it fitted in with the store."

"Meaning?"

"Just that. Unfortunately, I had to keep moving his week day shifts about."

"When did he ask you to enable him to go to therapy?"

"After he'd started. Daniel thought I could rig it just for him. Put his needs above everything and everyone else. Can you believe that?"

"Therapy is a legal right Mr Edmunds. You can't deny people who need it."

"I told him the shop had to come first. That he would have to sort something out for himself."

"How could he do that when you kept changing his shifts around?"

"That was just unfortunate. Hey, I've done nothing wrong. Why am I being interrogated?"

Rivers sighed. "You realise his defence will have a field day with all this? He may get off under mitigating circumstances. The jury may well be sympathetic to him."

"But assault is illegal."

"So is prejudice in the work place. So is denying someone with psychological problems treatment." Rivers' voice rose.

"I didn't know what his problems were."

"That's irrelevant. Don't you see? His defence will say he was pushed over the edge. I'll leave you to think this over, and talk to you another time."

Rivers turned to go.

"Hey Sergeant Rivers, people like Daniel Steele think the world owes them a living. Whose side are you on?" Edmunds demanded.

Rivers looked at him. "I'm just saying how it is."

Rivers stood before Spears, Walker and Burroughs, having just finished telling them his findings.

"The defence will love this." Spears sighed.

"Hold on. He still assaulted a man. CPS can't just drop charges for all we've heard," Walker put in.

"They won't." Burroughs explained. "But the defence will use this to the full."

"Use what?" Walker asked.

Rivers said, "He was special needs, and not only not getting support for it but getting a hard time about it from his colleagues. On its own that wouldn't be much of a defence. But the fact he was also denied access to therapy for what we can only assume was post-traumatic stress disorder will go strongly in his favour. They knew he had mental health problems and did sweet FA about it."

"It still doesn't justify what he did. We have the law to stop people bashing each other up left, right and centre and then claiming they'd been harassed into it, or blaming things like their parents' divorce when they were twelve for it. I got the impression Brian Lever was a prick, but that doesn't make it right what happened," Walker replied.

Before anything else could be said Superintendent Palmer stormed in. Palmer was six feet two in height, slender yet muscular with light brown hair and despite being young for his position had made a good first impression amongst the majority of police officers at Mansford.

"What's going on?" he demanded. "Why is it that I've had two complaints about this investigation? I've just had Robert Woods in my office wanting to know why his client is getting harassed at the gym, and Mark Edmunds just phoned me wanting to know whose side the investigating officer is on. Now would someone tell me what is going on?"

"Sir, if I may?" Burroughs said. "We had to visit Steele to let him know that we know his friends are potentially dangerous in this case. Four that we know of alone have previous convictions, so we will need to keep an eye on them."

"Also sir, I think Edmunds got the wrong end of the stick. I've found some things out, and I told him that this would work in Steele's favour." Rivers added.

"I see. So leaving that aside, if you believe Steele's friends to be a witness threat, what will you do?" Palmer asked.

"I favour a direct approach sir." Burroughs said. "I'd like to send Rivers and Walker into The Silver Seal pub to let Steele's friends know. I called the manager who said they're in there every week night between seven and nine. As we've spoken to Steele it's irrelevant whether he's there or not."

"Good." Palmer said. "If you two would like some overtime you could go this evening."

Both men nodded.

"For a Tuesday night it's busy." Walker commented.

"I'd say so. I heard this place is popular. Let's look out for – oh, look, Steele's here anyway." Rivers said.

"I recognise Redmond by his mug shot anyway." Walker replied. Let's say hello."

The group that included Ricky Ball and Alan Saunders and Matt Tyrell were laughing over a joke Pete had just made at Joe's expense. Ricky and Matt were about Daniel's age. Alan was in his mid-forties although he'd tell people he was in his late thirties.

"Yeah, yeah, yeah. Pick on me, that's what I'm here for." Joe smirked.

"Uh oh. Here come the boys who want to put me away," Daniel said, looking over.

"Yeah, you're so brave with your mates around you," Walker sneered.

"As you lot hide behind your position you can shut up!" Joe snapped.

"What are you doing here? He's doing no wrong." Pete demanded.

Rivers ignored him and said. "Daniel, you never said you were dyspraxic."

"What would it have meant if I had?"

"He was very unhappy in that job." Evan said.

"We all have hassle at work. Doesn't mean we can thump other people," Rivers said.

"Does if they deserve it," Pete snarled. "All those petty yobs and hoodies are out there vandalising, mugging. You don't worry about them."

"Because your hands are clean? Did that bloke you beat to a pulp deserve it?" Rivers demanded.

"He deserved a pasting but I admit I went over the top," Pete snapped.

"So how do you lot justify who gets it and who doesn't?" Rivers demanded.

"A bullying bastard gets no sympathy off any of us," Matt said.

"Who says he was a bully?" Walker asked. "Daniel here? Who is he to say?"

"I trust his word over some stranger's," Matt replied.

"How would you like it in a piss poor paid job where all you get is grief?" Rees demanded.

"I don't see how Daniel was much cop at anything. He had to accept what he could get and just get on with it," Walker said.

"Shut the fuck up!" Daniel snapped.

"Watch it sunbeam, or I'll have you in for offensive language at a police officer," Walker chided.

"That's enough," Rivers cut in. He addressed them all. "We want to let you know we know who you are. So don't be getting any ideas. If Brian Lever or any other witness has any accident or injury, you'll be our first suspects."

"Do you really think we're like that?" Pete demanded.

Outside Rivers gritted his teeth and kicked a bin.

"What's up, sarge? Something one of them said?" Walker asked.

"No, something you said to them. Telling Daniel Steele he should just accept what he could get."

"Yeah, so?"

"So that's what I used to have said to me. 'Just accept this is all you can ever do'."

"But you're a great detective."

"Don't you see? Steele was fucked off at being put down all the time. People with special needs are often intelligent. They just have trouble using it. Today Edmunds said quite calmly that Lever threw a box at Steele out of pure frustration. How often was that sort of thing going on? But no one cared. Because that's not illegal. Then Steele fights back, and that is."

"So are you special needs?"

Rivers stopped and stared at him. "I'm dyspraxic, alright? I always used to try hard, but got nowhere because of my problems. I used to get grief and putdowns from ignorant bastards who weren't much themselves, but used me to make them feel like more than they were."

TEN

Daniel met Woods after signing in for his bail.

"How are you Daniel?" Woods asked.

"OK, I guess. You?"

"Fine. Listen, I have to tell you that we'll be against a guy called George Hague."

"Know what he's like?"

"A colleague I spoke to said he's ruthlessly efficient."

"Nice guy, eh?"

"It's his job. Also, I've got DS Rivers leaning on me to take your statement."

"I'm ready. I'll do it."

"Be honest, is my advice. I will advise you on what not to answer."

Rivers and Walker came in. Rivers did the talking while Walker wrote.

"Right, Daniel." Rivers started. "You understand you have been charged with assault?"

"Yes."

"Do you admit to what you did?"

"No point denying it. I did."

"Are you going to plead guilty?"

"Don't answer that." Woods cut in.

"What else could you say?"

"Never mind." Woods said.

"All right then. You admit you did it. What happened?"

"He made me very angry, and I just flipped."

"Can you expand on that?"

"Yeah, the guy has been harassing me and picking on me since I started. At first I worked well, but after constant put downs and the Mickey Mouse shifts I was always doing, my morale really went downhill."

"Did you ever tell him about your problems?"

"I did. About the special needs. He abruptly replied 'I don't believe in them'. He used to start on me about going out and having a social life. I mean, the night before morning shift. I told him I had friends and liked to go out."

"What did he say?" Rivers asked

"That he didn't care. He used to tell me I was useless. That I should be grateful anywhere would have me."

"So, leading up to the assault, when you attacked him, how well do you remember that?"

"I was worked up that morning. The day before had been rough with some difficult customers and the previous Sunday I'd had lots of put-downs from Brian. I was dreading work the next day. When I arrived at work he told me straightaway he wasn't in the mood for any foul-ups, so I should keep out of his way. Then in the space of ten minutes he stomps through me so I had to jump out of his way. It was a power trip, you know?

"The assault itself was just a blur. All the things that make me angry just came out in those few seconds."

"Like the people in the supermarket calling you 'dyspastic'?" Rivers asked.

"Yeah, some of the managers and their suck-up crew. Look, I will try and think more about the attack. But I can't remember much now."

"Can we please end it here?" Woods asked.

"One more question," Rivers said. "The people we interviewed none spoke badly of Brian Lever like you did. Why is that?"

"People want a quiet life. There are people who don't like him."

After the interview Rivers and Walker went into Burroughs office where they found Lever with two other suited men.

"Bad timing. Steele's in the building," Walker commented.

"So what's he going to do?" Lever snapped.

Burroughs said, "This is George Hague, and this is Tony Partt, a Fast Service director."

Handshakes were exchanged.

"So these are our gallant boys that are responsible for putting a thug who assaulted a good man of ours away," Partt smiled.

"Hopefully," Rivers replied. "How's your back Mr Lever?"

"Sore. It hurts to bend over."

"We photographed the injuries," Walker explained.

"Do you reckon Steele's solicitor will try and keep them from being shown to the jury?" Hague asked.

"He could try, but he's more likely to try and downplay the extent," Rivers explained.

"Yes, the hospital has forwarded a report to me, and I asked to be kept updated," Hague said.

"Is Steele going to plead guilty?" Partt asked.

"I doubt it. He's aiming to go for mitigating circumstances." Walker replied.

"What?" Partt looked shocked.

"It's pointless him denying what he did, but he is aiming to prove he was driven to it." Rivers said.

"How does he reckon that?" Lever demanded.

"He claims, Mr Lever that you bullied and belittled him," Rivers said. "Is that true?"

"Of course not," Lever snapped.

"Did you know he was dyspraxic?"

"That sort of thing's an excuse for stupidity and laziness."

Rivers gritted his teeth and forced himself to stay calm. "Did you know he wanted to be in therapy for trauma issues, but was denied?"

"Not my problem. Can he really get off on this?"

"In this day and age of political correctness, it's possible, but unlikely." Hague said.

"His defence will use that combined with issues from what he went through when he was nineteen," Burroughs said.

"Which was?" Hague asked.

"He was pinned by three thugs and slashed up with a knife," Burroughs answered.

Hague nodded. "Thanks. I'll look into that. I'm guessing he brought it on himself."

"No," Burroughs told him. "I've checked it, and it was a case of mistaken identity. They thought he was someone who owed them drug money."

DC Cole knocked on the door. "Sorry ma'am, a Dr James McLeish is here, wanting to speak to someone about Daniel Steele."

Burroughs looked at Rivers. "Mike, can you?"

"Yes ma'am."

After Rivers left Hague said, "I'm looking to put him inside, let me assure you. If he gets off, this will open the door for people to assault their bosses and say they were pushed into it."

"I fail to see how any decent person could see him as a victim," Lever said angrily.

Rivers met Dr McLeish at the desk.

"Hi, I'm DS Mike Rivers."

"Dr James McLeish, I was Daniel Steele's psychologist. His solicitor phoned me yesterday and asked if I could help. Could I speak to you about him?"

"Yes, this way."

Rivers led McLeish into a vacant room and they sat.

"You have to understand, I'm not about to try and justify what Daniel did."

"I'm sure you're not."

"He's a very troubled young man. His learning disability frustrated him, he said. He worked hard, but had it held against him. That's just the start."

"Go on."

"Daniel suffered the usual symptoms of post-traumatic stress disorder: paranoia, fear of going out, sudden discomfort in social situations. But what troubled him most was paranoid obsessive thoughts he had."

"Another symptom of PTSD."

"Obsessive compulsive disorder. The two are linked"

"What, having to clean things again and again?"

"Not in this case. Fears that bad things would happen to people he cared about if he didn't do certain things. I can't breach patient confidentiality. So I can't say any more than that."

"You've told me a fair bit anyway. If you want to help him, you should tell all. Are you suggesting the assault was brought on by this? He's not registered as schizophrenic is he?"

"That's because he's not. Everything he was dealing with combined to push him too far. If he gives me permission I'll tell all."

"Too bad, he was here earlier. I could speak to his lawyer for you."

"Thanks, but I'll call him."

ELEVEN

It was Friday night. Daniel was out with his friends from the supermarket in neighbouring West Heyford. They were people he knew from working there and associated friends. They were talking and laughing as they left one pub to go to another.

"Hey!" His friend Jane called out. "There's Stu Berry. Hey Stuart!"

A tall slender man with black hair in his mid-twenties waved and jogged over. Daniel disliked him as he did Daniel, but, they had always left each other alone. Berry was a former colleague at the supermarket.

As Daniel walked he felt a slap to the left of his head and then a second to his right. He turned to see Berry smirking over him.

"Why'd you do that?" Daniel asked.

"Felt like it. Cut up any plastic chorizo's lately?"

"Shut up. That was four years ago and I gave it them 'cos I didn't care."

"That's not what I heard." Berry's breath smelt of alcohol. He turned to Jane. "Nice to see you guys. Pity this loser still tags along with you."

"I don't 'tag along' and I'm not a loser." Daniel said, fighting to stay calm. "So just fuck off you mug."

Berry reached forward to slap Daniel again. Daniel blocked it easily and stepped forward, pushing Berry back.

"You going to assault me like that old man are you?" Berry sneered.

"How – how do you know?" Daniel asked stunned.

"I know. They're going to put you inside where you'll get arse fucked."

"That's enough, Stu." Jane said.

Berry nodded. "See you all." He walked away.

"He does get lairy when he's had a few," a man called Dave said, shaking his head.

"Come off it," Daniel snapped. "He only starts on people who he figures won't fight back. See how he retreated when I pushed him?"

"There was no call for that," Jane told him.

"And what he said was all right was it?" Daniel demanded.

"Well you did cut up that plastic chorizo," Jane laughed.

"And for that reason people like him think I'll always be a failure."

"Oh, Daniel. You'll never live that down." She grinned.

"You think that justifies the treatment I get? Why d'you think I kicked off at work?"

"What you did there was wrong." A girl called Bryony chimed in.

Daniel stopped walking. "What is this? Gang up on me night?"

"How do you justify beating a 57 year old up?" Bryony demanded.

"I'll tell you." They were at a bus stop and Daniel waved at an approaching bus. "Because of the ignorance I have to deal with. Fuck this. I'm going home!"

He got on the bus and paid for a ticket, sat down and didn't even look at his friends as they passed.

Daniel did not go home. He got off in Mansford and walked to his local, The Duke. Walking in he said 'all right' to the familiar faces, but was looking for and hoping to see one. He found her having a cigarette in the garden.

"Hi, Michelle," he said, forcing a smile.

"You OK? You look upset."

Michelle Fielder was ten years older, an attractive woman of medium build with blonde hair just past her shoulders. During Daniel's previous period of unemployment they had struck up a close friendship. Michelle was happily married with three young children so things would go no further. But they were both content that way.

"Last thing I needed tonight. I went out with some of my lot from when I worked at the supermarket. I got into a confrontation with a bloke I used to work with. He just started on me.

"Of course everyone thinks he's a great guy, and the girls fancy him; probably why they took his side. I pushed him, nothing more. But it's the attitude of his to just accept I'm a failure. It was all about that plastic chorizo incident."

"I think you told me. What happened again?"

"When I was new at the supermarket I was left on my own to close down the deli counter. It was still busy though. One time I was so strung out while I was putting everything away. This couple kept harassing me for chorizo. I kept telling them we have none.

"After a while they pointed to the hams and salamis at the back hanging off and tell me it's there. So I cut them a chunk. I find out the next day what it was – plastic, fake. Obviously I get a fair bit of grief about it for a while, but I let it slide. But now if I'm made out to be a failure and I try to talk about how I feel, someone like Jane reminds me of it. She's got no work ambitions and thinks I should be the same."

"So this guy who started on you, who was he? That's what he brings up?"

"Stuart Berry. First time I met him he started about it. He made out he wanted to be friends, but figured, probably because of my size I was just some bitch boy to be picked on. He's not much himself, build wise. As time went on and I gave him a lot of verbal back and we fell out."

"Do you get a lot of grief about the chorizo incident?"

"The managers who saw me as 'attitudy' and their kiss-up crew would every now and then. They were the types that liked to pick on those they saw as insecure.

"But what gets to me more is the way people like my friend Jane use it on me when I'm worked up. Like when a woman at work said I was too 'dippy' to ever get anywhere and Jane just smirked and said 'Well, you did cut up a plastic chorizo.

"And then people wonder why I get so worked up, it's wrong what I did, and it could put me inside, which I admit, worries me, but do those ignorant bastards not realise this is why people lose their motivation?"

She held his hand. "If it would help you, you know I'm prepared to speak for you in court."

"Thanks, that means something." He managed to smile. "Now let's forget it and have a laugh."

TWELVE

Lever returned to work the next Tuesday. He had not been signed off by the doctor but came back on the condition stated by Edmunds that he did light duties. Edmunds had already opened the shop up and people who liked Brian cheered when he arrived.

"Don't worry, no one's spoken against you here," one woman assured him.

Lever looked over at Stacey and Adam who were opening and putting out bundles of newspapers.

"I'm not sure," Brian said.

He walked out the back to find Edmunds.

"Good to have you back," Edmunds said. "How do you feel?"

"Back plays up a bit. Listen, what do you reckon was said to the police about me?"

"Don't worry, the staff only spoke badly of Daniel. As for the two he requested, I took them into the office and told them I'd sack them if they said anything they shouldn't."

"I assume Adam and Stacey?"

"Yeah, I have to keep things looking good in my interests. I don't need the area manager giving me grief. I don't like you, any more than you do me, but I do respect you, and as long as you show me respect, I'll remain on your side." He smiled.

Brian nodded. The threat was unspoken, but clear.

At half-past seven the same morning Pete and Joe walked in to the store. Joe was doing some temporary cash in hand work for Pete.

"Hope you're ready to work today Joe, I don't want to be tying cow bells around your neck again," Pete said.

"That was humiliating. I don't want that again," Joe smiled embarrassed.

"Yeah, well don't skive off on cigarette breaks and it won't happen," Pete replied.

They got a soft drink each and some crisps and put them on a till. The young man with 'Adam' on his name badge served them.

"You were a mate of Daniel's weren't you?" Joe asked.

Adam nodded.

"Raw deal he got eh?" Pete said.

"Adam – stop talking to them right now!" Brian snapped, striding over.

Pete pulled himself up to his full height. At six feet he towered eight inches over Brian.

"You go away, no one's talking to you," Pete said patronizingly to Brian. He smiled at Adam, and said, "He's a tosser isn't he?" Adam just smiled nervously.

"If you've made your purchases leave now!" Brian said angrily.

At the same height as Pete, Joe also towered over Brian.

"Shut up you fucking little grass," Joe snapped. "All that shit you give Daniel and then you kick off because he reacts."

"He attacked me!" Brian snarled.

"I've had far worse than a punch in the gob and a push you little twat!" Joe yelled.

"I wonder why," Brian growled.

"What did you say?" Joe stepped forward. Pete grabbed his shoulder and pulled him back. Pete then stood over Brian. He smiled patronizingly.

"Who's the cute little man? Hello little man," he said in a patronising tone. Brian stood his ground with his teeth gritted, trying to maintain his dignity.

Joe, smiling now stepped forward and patted Brian on the head. "What a funny looking little man you are," he said, imitating Pete.

"Get – out!" Brian ordered.

Pete bent over close to the floor. "Did someone say something?" Then he made eye contact with Brian. "Oh, there."

"Get – out!" Brian repeated.

"All right." Pete said normally. "By the way, Daniel doesn't know we did this. So don't go whinging to the police." Pete and Joe walked out.

Brian turned on Adam. "What were you thinking?" he demanded.

"What could I have done?" Adam asked feebly.

"Gone and got Mark, told them to leave. Not just stood like a statue."

"It was just so fast. I'm sorry, Brian."

Brian glared at him and then turned and walked away.

Daniel walked to the police station. After signing in he was taken to meet Woods. Woods was in the room with another young man in a suit. Medium height and build, with glasses and light brown hair.

"Thank you, constable." Woods smiled at the officer who had led Daniel in. The police man nodded and went out, closing the door. "Daniel, this is Gary Brooks, the barrister."

"Good to meet you," Daniel smiled, shaking his hand.

"Likewise." Brooks smiled. "We need to talk Daniel. Let's sit down."

They did, and then Woods spoke.

"I had a phone call from George Hague. He made it clear to me he wants to put you away for a bit, to 'set an example'."

"People do worse than me, and get let off with cautions," Daniel said stunned. He felt sick to hear what Woods had just said.

"It's a case of showing the law has zero tolerance for people who assault their bosses." Brooks explained.

"I am all for that, but I was driven to it."

"As I told Hague. He laughed and said 'You try and prove that.' Daniel, the plea you make is a fair way away, and I am genuinely on your side, but as Hague says, how can we prove it with no one' backing you up?"

"You think I should plead guilty?"

"If no one is prepared to back your story up you can do that and make out you acted as a result of trauma. Remember you get bonus points as it were, for pleading in time."

"No one will speak for me because Mark Edmunds threatened to sack them if they did. I reckon that's why or something like that."

"How do we prove that?" Brooks asked.

"Look Daniel, I need you to think carefully here." Woods said seriously. "Are you prepared to try this? Because it would be a serious case of witness intimidation if true. It will be investigated, but if it can't be proven it will reflect very badly on you."

"What have I got to lose? I'm screwed without someone to back me up." Daniel replied.

"All right." Woods nodded. "I'll speak to DI Burroughs later. I'll get it checked out."

That evening Rivers and Walker found themselves walking into The Silver Seal again. They saw Daniel at the bar alone.

"In here a lot these days aren't you? Or is it coincidence?" Walker asked.

"Coincidence. This is looking like harassment," Daniel said irritably.

"So is what some friends of yours did this morning," Rivers told him.

"I had nothing to do with it, whatever it was,"

"We're supposed to believe that," Walker smirked.

"Yes," Pete said walking back from the toilets. "Two of us went in there and I couldn't resist having a dig."

"It's called witness harassment," Rivers said. "Now leave us to talk to Daniel."

"What? So you can push him into saying something he shouldn't?"

"We can talk here or take him to the station. And if you lot continue to harass Brian Lever I'll have you on a charge of harassment and might even look into revoking Daniel's bail," Rivers said.

Pete looked at Daniel. "Me and Evan are outside," he said.

"You'd better talk to us," Rivers said.

"After what you just threatened to have done to me?"

"We have to protect the victim. It seems your friends are taking this personally," Rivers said.

"Do you blame them? The way I was treated there."

"You knew the sort of shifts you'd have to do when you started," Walker pointed out.

"All right, I can't argue that, but it was more than I could handle. I got worn out and frustrated after months of it."

Neither detective showed any emotion.

"Given a hard time were you?" Rivers asked. "Being dyspraxic, a slow learner. People aren't too sympathetic."

"You patronizing bastard. Like you'd understand," Daniel gasped.

"Oh I would. I am too," Rivers said.

"Only he doesn't have those problems," Walker added.

Rivers glared at his colleague, and raised his hand for silence.

Daniel forced a grin. "Am I meant to buy this? Trying to make me believe that one of you is all sympathetic. The old good cop, bad cop routine is it, guys?"

"So Brian Lever gave you a hard time, verbally pushes you, and finally you snap," Rivers pressed.

"Hey, I admitted to what I did. What more do you want?"

"To understand; to realise what pushed you over the edge. I know what happened when you were eighteen. About the knife attack," Rivers said.

"Those things combined don't help. If you're dyspraxic you should understand what it's like to be patronised and put down and made to feel like you can never be anything. Not just that, but, my lack of size means I should just accept being a victim. Am I supposed to be like Adam Chester? No self-esteem. Just because society says it should be that way," Daniel blurted out.

Walker stepped forward. "So that's how it is. Blame society, blame this and that for your own failings. That's how it always is with your kind," he growled.

"Chris," Rivers snapped. Walker looked at him and stepped back.

"Guess I was wrong. I thought I could talk to you guys. Unless there's anything else I'm going to go." Daniel stormed off outside.

The two detectives walked outside. Walker suddenly stepped around facing Rivers.

"What was that sarge?" he demanded. "Tell me you were playing him because I can't just believe it was anything else."

"Stand down," Rivers said.

"Look, we're police. Do not tell me you sympathise with that thug."

"He's no thug, all right? He lost it for a minute."

"That's how they talk. As he said, he admitted it, what he did. Let his defence handle the sympathy side. You never attacked anyone for giving you a hard time."

"No, but I wanted to."

"Look, sarge, we're the law. Sometimes it does feel that the perpetrators were pushed into it, but you side with Daniel Steele today, the next thing we know you'll be siding with a thief because he got into debt or a drug addict because they had a hard life. We can't think that way."

Rivers sighed. "You're right. Just a moment of weakness I guess. Thanks."

"It's OK. We all have those moments. You're just lucky I was here to kick you into line. He grinned and Rivers returned it.

THIRTEEN

DI Burroughs had Rivers and Walker in her office the next day.

"An interesting allegation from Robert Woods," she said. "A claim that Mark Edmunds may have intimidated staff to stay silent by threats of dismissal."

"You think he's clutching at straws?" Walker asked

"Possibly. I told him we'd look into it."

"There's only one way to prove it and that's to either turn up unannounced or talk to Adam Chester or Stacey Willis out of the store," Rivers said.

"For all we know though Steele may have sneakily coaxed them," Burroughs pointed out.

"We'll have to turn up unannounced then, only send DC Spears; I'm not very popular with Edmunds," Rivers said. "Also they won't recognise him if he goes in first."

At mid-day Spears walked into the store leaving Walker two minutes up the road, waiting for his missed call signal to come in. The store was busy, staff putting stock out. No sign of Lever or Edmunds. Spears stopped one young man.

"Excuse me sir," he said. and showed his warrant card, making sure no other staff were watching. "DC Spears, I'm on the Daniel Steele case."

"What's to tell, he did it, didn't he? Attacked Brian, but to be fair I know I wouldn't mind."

"Really? We were given the impression Brian was well respected here."

"Yeah, by some. A fair few dislike the bloke. I'm a morning porter stroke supervisor like him and if things aren't done his way and to his satisfaction he's always on your case."

"What about Adam Chester, and Stacey Willis they neither spoke badly of him."

The man looked around nervously. "Look, Mark told any of us who liked Daniel and not Brian to keep our gobs shut or he'd sack us, or make our lives harder. Him and Brian can't stand each other, but it saves Mark trouble, and means he can blackmail Brian by saying he helped him out."

"What's your name?"

"Jimmy Hatton."

"Are you prepared to help us?"

"It'd be my pleasure." Hatton smiled.

"When you finish the shift, would you be prepared to meet me at the station? Ask for DC Spears."

"Yes, I finish at two, I'll be there."

Spears did not bother to call Walker, but instead just left the store and met him.

"I got someone." Spears said.

"You what?"

"Looks like Daniel got lucky. Edmunds has been intimidating people into staying quiet."

When Hatton came in to the station he said he was not working with Edmunds again until Saturday morning. He willingly listened to the instructions Spears gave him and accepted a tape recorder.

FOURTEEN

On the Thursday evening Daniel turned down an invite by Joe and Matt, to go to Matt's house. Instead he arrived at The Cart and Horse pub for a former colleague at the supermarket's retirement party. He turned up and was welcomed by people who had liked him, but some shunned him. He ignored them.

"So Margaret, retirement at last." He smiled at the woman retiring.

"Oh yes. And worth it I can tell you. Me and my husband have some grand plans," she said.

Nearby a lanky red headed young man and a short blonde middle aged woman looked at him distastefully.

"How can he be so welcome here?" the red head asked angrily.

"He knows how to charm people, as he did when he worked with us," the woman grumbled.

For two hours the conversation was upbeat, and Daniel was more relaxed than he had been in a while. Then Adam Jackson, a short, fat man in his early twenties kept taunting a special needs man called Andy.

"Can't you leave the poor guy alone?" Daniel asked.

"No, he doesn't mind, like little Sam here," Jackson chuckled reaching over and slapping Sam, a small timid young man, around the head.

Daniel smiled. "That's not nice," he said.

"You don't mind do you Sam?" Jackson asked.

"No, no I don't," Sam said nervously.

"You see, Daniel. Anyway, this coming from someone who beat up a man thirty years older." He looked to his teen lackeys, who smiled, not really wanting to get involved.

"Please. Don't start," Daniel pleaded.

"Or when you cut up that plastic chorizo," Jackson continued. Sniggers followed.

"Flip the record, Jackson. That's all you ever use on me," Daniel said.

"Well, now I can call you the granddad basher I guess," Jackson laughed.

"You know something?" Daniel snapped. "Your gob is like your gut, too much of it and a waste of space!"

"That's an appalling thing to say!" Adam's girlfriend Hanna said stunned.

"And the things your boyfriend says and does to insecure people isn't?" Daniel demanded.

"He's only messing about!" she said angrily.

"Watch it. He might beat you up too," the red head sneered.

"You saying I'd bash up a girl, Alec!" Daniel shouted. "I'll punch YOU cunt!"

The blonde woman Alec was next to said, "A sad little nothing. That's all you are Daniel. I know how slow you are to pick things up and your mental problems. We all have them, but you're too weak to handle them."

"Shut up," Daniel growled.

"The bad things that happened to you were your own fault," she continued.

"They were not!"

"You're going to go nowhere. You're stupid, a nuisance, not to mention a skinny little nothing!" She smirked.

"Shut it you, poisoned dwarf!" Daniel roared. "That's what people call you. You're the most despised person in that supermarket Stella."

Stella started to whimper. "That's not true."

"You say things about people, and then don't even have the courage to admit it when you get found out. You just lie and say it was someone else!"

"Has anyone ever told you what a horrible little man you are?" she sobbed.

The bar manager came over. He asked Stella, "Are you all right?"

"He upset her, and threatened me," Alec snarled.

"You'll have to leave, sir, or I'll have to call the police," the manager said.

"Yeah, you should," Stella said tearfully as Alec consoled her. He looked distastefully at Daniel.

"You just look at me that way, fag boy," Daniel said, emotions choking him. "And you, you nasty bitch," he said. to Stella.

He glared at Jackson who pulled himself back. "Just a cowardly bully aren't you? Always putting people down. Take a look in the mirror sometime."

He stormed outside and continued walking until he reached a bench and sat down breathing deeply to combat the swirling emotions, reminders of his bad treatment by Jackson and the two managers he sucked up to, Elaine who he had worked with telling him he was too 'dippy' to ever get anywhere in life.

He dug out his phone and dialled Joe. "Does that offer still apply?" he asked.

Daniel got a bus to Mansford and then a taxi to Matt's house. Matt let him in. Matt shared a house with his landlord and a young couple. In Matt's room Joe was already drunk.

"Hey Daniel," he slurred. "I thought you had that party tonight."

"I did. But I was turfed out. For sticking up for myself and a couple of shy blokes. Some people there think they have the right to judge me."

"For socking that bastard you worked with?" Matt asked.

"Fucking cunt. He deserved it and more," Joe growled.

"It sounds bad when some tosser called me a 'granddad basher'. You know. Maybe I should feel bad. But I don't," Daniel sighed.

"Why – the fuck should you feel bad?" Joe asked.

"The guy was always giving you a hard time and that. I hear you, but don't feel bad. Here," Matt put a beer can in his hand.

They were knocking back cans and listening to music. Daniel found himself drunk and giggling as Matt pointed out a spill stain to Joe.

"Er, Joe, look what you did," Matt said. "See that stain?"

"Yeah. Oh sorry, did I spill my drink?"

"No, you pissed yourself there," Matt said.

Joe, as drunk as he was, half believed it.

"No, don't fuck with me," he slurred.

"Hey, I'm not angry with you Joe, I'm just saying. Look what you did."

"No, I never did, tell me it's a wind up. It's not funny."

Matt grinned. "All right, it is, but look at Daniel. That's the happiest I've seen him in a long time."

"Yeah, you're one of ours," Joe told Daniel. "Now I do need to piss."

Daniel and Matt sat listening to the music when they suddenly heard,

"What are you doing walking in like that?" A man's voice shouted out.

"Oh sorry, mate, should have locked the door," Joe said loudly.

"The locks broke dumb arse. That's why the sign says 'Knock'."

"Don't call me that," Joe snarled.

"Oh great," Matt smiled wryly.

Matt and Daniel ran upstairs to find Joe confronting Matt's house mate, Kevin.

"Fucking speak to me like that," Joe said.

Daniel got in between them.

"Leave it," he said. Matt grabbed Kevin.

"Come on, not here," he said, guiding Kevin into Kevin's room. "Do your piss, he" called back to Joe,

"Fucking prick, speak to me like that," Joe said angrily.

"Just leave it eh?" Daniel smiled.

Back in Matt's room they continued to drink. Then Matt's landlord Kyle walked in.

"Hey guys, do you think I could filch a couple of beers?" He pulled out a small see through bag. "I got something in it for you guys." "Help yourself," Matt smiled, accepting the bag. Kyle nodded, taking three bottles and giving Matt the bag.

"Coke?" Daniel asked.

Joe nodded. "Want some?"

"Nah, not this time, eh."

Daniel watched his friends snort the coke. He had never done it, but had to wonder, how long until he did.

Just after nine am, Saturday morning, Daniel woke up, sprawled on Matt's floor. He had covered himself with his own coat, and used a cushion taken from the living room for his pillow. In the kitchen he could hear Joe talking to Kevin.

"Sorry about all that last night, I was a bit bent out of shape," Joe said.

"It's ok. Me too," Kevin replied.

"Good mate of mine's being charged with beating up some bastard he worked with. It should be that bloke on trial for treating people like he did."

Two hours later, they were all up and decided to head into town. On the way they walked past the hardware store Daniel had worked at. Outside stood the owner, Roger, and also Miles Booth, a sales assistant that had disliked Daniel for his problems.

"Morning gents," Daniel smiled.

"Morning," Roger replied.

"Hear you lost your job at Fast Service?" Miles said disdainfully.

"Yeah, I did," Daniel replied.

"For assault on an old boy."

"True, I just lost it for a bit, you know."

"So, you'll be back on benefits again. Taking my taxes." Miles glared at him.

"Until I get something else, what choice have I got?"

"Not to get in these situations," Miles said bluntly.

Still drunk, and aggressive from the cocaine, Joe stepped forward. "Shut the fuck up. He doesn't want to be on fifty quid a week, any more than you want him on it."

"No excuse for being on the dole. Anyone on it is a sponging bastard to me," Miles replied.

"I'm on incapacity," Joe snarled.

"You're still a sponging bastard then," Miles replied.

"You fucking what?" Joe demanded. "You wanna lose your teeth, faggot?"

"Get inside," Roger ordered Miles, and the two went inside.

"Leave it," Matt told Joe.

"He's a sad prick with no social life, kind of pitiful really," Daniel said.

Joe nodded and walked along, then suddenly stopped and ran back. He threw the door open and stormed up to Miles. Standing right up to him, he shouted,

"You ever mouth off at me or a mate of mine again, I'll break you, you little fuck."

He then spat in Miles' face and stormed back out.

FIFTEEN

Jimmy Hatton watched Edmunds walking around the store, talking pleasantly to those he liked, and chiding those he didn't.

"Adam, make yourself useful for once! You're putting out sweets, it's not hard, move faster!" Edmunds snapped. Adam nodded and continued his job.

Paul Hirst who had started on the day of the attack looked at Jimmy.

"On the war path isn't he?" Paul smiled.

"Don't let him worry you, he's a prick. By the way, are you going to give evidence against Daniel?" Jimmy asked.

"If they need me."

"Daniel should have done more."

"You can't go around assaulting people."

"Maybe not, but I figured someone would lose it with Brian one day."

"Why?"

"Because Brian's an obnoxious arrogant bastard who thinks it's OK to bollock you about every piddly little thing."

"I guess he has high standards."

"It's more of a power trip with him."

"Jimmy," Edmunds called out. "You wanted to talk to me."

"Yeah, just need the toilet, then I'll speak to you in the office."

Jimmy went into the toilet as he had planned. He took the tape recorder out of his left trouser pocket and set it to 'record'. He then put it back in his pocket and walked in to Edmunds' office. He closed the door.

"What can I do for you?" Edmunds asked.

"I wanted to talk to you about the police investigation. I wanted to speak for Daniel Steele, and say what a tosser Brian is."

"You can speak for Daniel, but not against Brian."

"Or what? You'll sack me, like you threatened to do to Adam and Stacey?"

"I need you. I won't sack you, but you will find your life will get harder here."

Jimmy had been told he needed a direct admission. "So you'll make my life harder?" Edmunds nodded, to his irritation. "Say it. You'll make my life harder."

"I said things would get harder. You think Brian or anyone who respects him would respond too well to it?"

"So why did you threaten to sack people if they talked?"

"Who said I did?"

"It's common knowledge."

"I'm just trying to maintain a good working environment here Jimmy."

Jimmy felt frustrated. But then he thought of something to really aggravate Edmunds.

"Or to keep Brian off your case. Get him on your side."

Edmunds shot up. "Get out!" he shouted.

"You just want to keep the trouble down, so you threaten shy people like Stacey and Adam with their jobs," Jimmy snarled.

Edmunds lowered his tone. "I've got to keep things going here. Daniel was a fucking nuisance. So is Brian, but I do what I have to."

"So you threaten people to stay quiet?"

Finally Edmunds said it. "Yes, I did. Do you know why? Because otherwise I'll have an inquiry into how things are. Better to just let Daniel go to prison, and let it go there."

"What if the police found out? You'd be screwed."

"How would they? If anyone told them I'd deny it. Does anyone really care about people like Adam and Stacey who will never get anywhere? I told them I'd sack them, and if you decide to blab, then I'll see to it Brian and his fan club knows you sided with a whining thug like Daniel, now get out."

Jimmy smiled. "Thanks for seeing me."

Woods had been talking to another client at the police station. He was just clearing up his paperwork when he was aware of a man standing over him.

"Robert Woods I presume," the well-spoken man said.

"That's right."

The man extended a hand. "George Hague. I'm the prosecutor in the Steele case."

Woods accepted the hand shake.

"So, how can I help you, Mr Hague?"

"I wanted to explain some things to you. Understand; this is not official. I just thought I'd have a chat."

"And you must understand, it could be considered unethical."

"As I say, it's not official. You can leave if you want."

Woods clasped his hands. "Go on."

"You must see, the odds are in my favour all the way. A 24 -year -old assaults a man over thirty years his senior for telling him off."

"After constant harassment and put downs."

"Says your client. Who is confirming that?"

"No one yet."

"I doubt anyone will either. Mr Lever is a highly respected and dedicated worker. The company that employs him feels that it is owed it to him to prosecute Steele to the full extent of the law. Also as a prosecutor I feel it necessary to set an example. To show the public that we show zero tolerance to those who assault their superiors."

"I see. So what is your point?"

"I intend to put your client in prison. Not for a long time, but long enough. There will be no plea bargain. It will be a simple case of him pleading guilty immediately, and he will do roughly five months, or him pleading not guilty and being sentenced to double that. That's how I imagine the judge will see it"

"Right."

Hague smiled pleasantly. "Does that 'right' indicate your agreement?"

"No, I've something else in mind."

"Yes?" Hague's smile stayed.

"You see, I'm planning to show to the public zero tolerance to victimisation in the workplace. That mistreatment of people with special needs should not be allowed, and that people in authority do not have the right to patronise and bully. And also people with psychiatric problems such as the PTSD my client suffers from, should be allowed access to treatment as unsupported they can spin out of control."

Hague leaned on the table. "Let me be frank, Mr Woods. You are only thirty-two. I am forty nine, all my working life in working law. Nearly twenty years difference in experience. You are, pardon the phrase, an office boy in comparison. Do you not think I can find my way around every little thing you intend to use?"

Arrogant bastard, Woods thought. He stood up, and opened his mouth, but at that moment Rivers charged in.

"There you are, Woods. Hague, what are you doing here? Never mind. I'm glad you are, I need to speak with both of you."

Rivers led them to the CID offices. Walker and Spears stood there grimly. Spears held a tape recorder.

"What is this?" Hague asked.

"This will change a fair few things," Spears replied. He pressed 'play'.

After it finished Hague asked "So this changes what?"

"It means we can't find credibility in the witnesses we've had," Rivers replied. "We have to assume Mark Edmunds has launched a major cover up to suit himself. Now this has come to light it's done Brian Lever no favours."

"He had nothing to do with it," Hague said.

"No, but it means we'll have to interview the entire staff there," Rivers said.

"After arresting and removing Mark Edmunds," Walker added.

"Is that necessary?" Hague asked.

"I'm afraid so," Rivers said. "He's messed us all around."

"We'll need to remove him quickly and quietly, so staff feel they can speak freely."

"Another client for you," Woods remarked. Hague ignored him.

"You'd better contact Tony Partt after we've done this, let him know," Rivers told Hague. "Please stay with my colleagues for now."

"Why?" Hague asked.

"We don't want to risk Partt discovering now and warning Edmunds," Walker explained.

Twenty minutes later Rivers entered the store with two uniformed officers. He asked to be taken to Edmunds and walked into the office without knocking. Edmunds saw him and stood.

"DS Rivers, I'm very busy at the moment," he said.

"Have you a supervisor you can put in charge?" Rivers asked.

"Yes, why?"

"Things have come out. Mark Edmunds, I am arresting you on suspicion of witness intimidation and attempting to pervert the course of justice. You do not have to say anything now, but it may harm your defence if you fail to mention something now you later rely on in court. Do you understand?"

"No. Why am I being arrested?"

"For your attempts to silence witnesses. We have strong evidence against you, threatening people with their jobs if they speak about certain things you want kept quiet. There's no need to make a fuss. Just tell your main supervisor that you have to go with us and that they are to take over," Rivers told him.

"Right," Edmunds glared at Rivers.

They followed him out.

"Amjad, I have to go with these guys to talk about the case. Take over please."

Edmunds was led out to a car and put in.

"This disgusts me," he snarled.

SIXTEEN

Miles Booth sat before Rivers and Walker later that day in an interview room.

"I understand your anger, but you have to understand how it looks," Rivers said.

"Daniel is an idiot. He probably wanted his friend to do that," Miles snapped.

"We can't prove that. I know uniform spoke to a witness who said you provoked Steele by going on about him being on benefits. And Joe McGinty. Who by the way has no previous for violence."

"No, I was just stating a fact. I'm a man of principles. A rare thing these days. As I'm like that I believe in upholding my principles. People like Daniel and that friend of his, Joe, will be offended because they violate them."

"You worked with Daniel didn't you?"

"Yes and he was so slow to pick things up it was unbelievable."

"Is that why he was dismissed?"

"Roger had had enough. He needs people to learn quicker. But he wanted to help Daniel. He suggested Daniel check out a petrol station where all he'd have to do was sit on a till all day. Even Daniel could do that."

"You think that's right?"

"I think people like him should accept that's all they can get. But no, Daniel was unemployed for a long time. Said he was doing courses with the skills centre. And because he was in treatment for mental health problems he got to go on that incapacity benefit. He came in one day to talk to a friend. I told him to stop taking our taxes. That he should get a job, whatever it was and stop sponging on benefits. He said. he was in therapy. I said 'just deal with things like we all have to'."

"So then he got the job at Fast Service?"

"Yeah, Roger had said to him when he was in his final period of employment that he should see if there were any jobs there as well, and I also think those places will take anyone."

"It made him worse. Do you think he bears you any ill feelings, Mr Booth?" Rivers asked.

"He will do. I used to make my feelings clear to him. Can you imagine how frustrating it was dealing with someone who took so long to pick things up?"

"Did he try?" Rivers asked.

"Does it matter? He couldn't do it."

"I'd advise caution. Technically that is called harassment," Rivers told him.

"What?"

"Getting on someone's case because they struggle."

"I don't believe it is."

"Don't get me wrong, I will see to it that they don't harass you again," Rivers told him.

"How can it be that it's wrong to get frustrated at morons like Daniel?"

"I used to be one of those!" Rivers snapped. "I had to deal with prejudice and discrimination, and look where I am! A detective-sergeant. Because I found my calling. And with the right support he could too."

"Next time, I want them charged," Miles snapped and walked out.

It didn't surprise Rivers that Burroughs asked to see him.

"Miles Booth has made a complaint against you for giving him attitude," she said.

"The man is obnoxious and ignorant. It's people like him that push people like Steele over the edge," Rivers said angrily.

"There's NO excuse for what they do," Burroughs said coldly.

"It's hard for me ma'am, when I hear people with learning difficulties referred to like that."

"My son is dyslexic, he doesn't have problems learning."

"That's the problem isn't it? Not all special needs cases are the same."

"I'm surprised at your attitude. You will go to Major Hardware and apologise in person to Miles Booth sometime tomorrow."

SEVENTEEN

Walker went into The Silver Seal that night. He saw Joe, Pete and Evan. He approached them.

"You're becoming a regular," Pete grunted.

"Cut the shit, I heard what your boys got up to," Walker told him.

"What was that then?" Pete asked.

Walker looked at Joe. "Spitting in a man's face."

"So nick me. Daniel did nothing illegal," Joe replied.

"If you really care about your mate you lot will behave. We've got you for giving grief to the victim."

"Victim, don't make me laugh," Evan cut in.

"You think he deserved it?"

"Fuckin' yeah. You don't go pissing about like that and then go crying 'cos you get bit," Evan said.

"Daniel's plea is coming up. Any more bad behaviour and I'll see to it that it comes back on him," Walker snapped.

"Is that a threat?" Joe demanded.

"It's a promise," Walker said, and walked away.

"Fucker," Joe said quietly.

Daniel was in The Duke with Michelle and his friend Graham. So too were Sean Mortimer and Adam Jackson. With them were some others.

"Those two, Sean and Adam, two managers at the supermarket I was at. That lot with them are the 'suck-up' crew I said about," Daniel explained.

"How's the 'dyspastica' Daniel?" One yelled. Sniggers came up.

"Fine Tim, just like your mum was when I left her last night," Daniel smiled.

"Hey!" Hanna yelled. "That's going too far."

"I don't think so," Daniel said. Inside the anger was building.

"Watch out for the oldie basher," Sean cracked.

"Hey guys, let it go," Graham called out.

"They're really brave when they're together, get one on their own and the confidence goes," Daniel said to his friends.

"I'm going out the back for a cigarette, come on," Michelle said.

The three went outside and continued talking. Then Sean and Adam came out.

"To what do I owe the pleasure?" Daniel asked.

"Just wanted to make sure you weren't going to gang-bang the lady here against her will," Sean cracked, nodding at Michelle.

Graham saw Michelle step back, looking confused. Daniel lowered his head.

"Shut up Sean," he said firmly.

"Hey, Daniel, let's face it the only way a little bloke with a receding hair line like you can get laid is to rape someone," Sean continued a big grin on his face.

What happened next happened was too fast for Graham to think. Daniel suddenly lunged forward. His right hand grabbed Sean around the throat. The left to the scruff of Sean's jumper. He slammed Sean against the wall. Not powerful grips, but enough to shock Sean. Jackson was too stunned to move.

"Shut – the- fuck – UP!" Daniel shouted.

"Hey – uh – let go," Sean gasped.

"Feeling brave enough to step in Jackson," Daniel demanded.

Jackson stood there. Graham, big man that he was just stood, open mouthed.

"Please Daniel," Michelle begged.

Daniel suddenly relaxed and let go. Sean staggered to the side, gasping.

"Get outta here," Daniel snarled. "You snitch on me, I'll set some friends of mine on you. If you don't believe me, find out."

Still gasping, Sean staggered inside, followed by the stunned Jackson.

"What did you do that for?" Graham asked.

"He's got a big mouth and he runs it off too much," Daniel replied.

"Your plea is in three days mate. If they snitch on you-" Graham started.

"I know. I'll go inside," Daniel said nervously. "I just lost it for a bit."

"Could we please have a minute?" Michelle asked Graham.

He nodded and went inside. Daniel looked at Michelle. Her eyes moist.

"I hate violence," she said.

"You're thinking about what happened to you, aren't you?" Daniel said.

"Yes. I knew those."

"I know. You don't have to tell me. I'm sorry. That was what was going through my head. I was thinking about you."

"You still shouldn't have done that. I'm scared you'll go to prison if he doesn't take your threat seriously."

"I'm worried too." They hugged each other.

The next day was tense for Daniel. Several times when he was at home he thought he heard the police coming for him. At two he heard the doorbell ring and went to answer it. Woods stood there.

"You all right, Daniel?"

"All right, mate. Come in."

He made himself and Woods tea and they sat down to talk.

"I've some very good news for you," Woods smiled.

"What? Brian dropped the charges?"

"I'm afraid not. But Mark Edmunds got arrested when it was proved he was intimidating witnesses. It means he's been removed from his job, and the police can now get to the truth. Two people have already come forward and said you were a good guy and Brian is a bully."

"So I can plead not guilty then?"

Woods looked serious. "Yes, you can. I'll need your former psychologist to testify. And we'll bring up former colleagues who are on your side and not intimidated by Brian Lever. Here's where I'm worried though. George Hague approached me and made it clear he wants to put you away to 'set an example'."

"But far worse than me -"

"I know. But this guy is an arrogant tosser. He wants to keep in with CPS. He's offered five months inside if you plead guilty on the day."

"And if I don't?"

"Up to a year. His words. It's up to the judge of course, not him. But he will lean on her. By the way, we've got Judge Abigail Nolan," Woods told him.

"What's she like?"

"A good one. She doesn't lean either to the prosecution or defence in terms of favouritism – like a lot do. She has no time for theatrics."

Daniel grinned. "Can you get me off?"

"I won't make any promises. In my mind, a lawyer that promises that is a fool."

"But you'll try your best?"

"Of course. I think I can put up a good fight. There are things in our favour, and things against us. If you plead not guilty I'll claim diminished responsibility, and I will make Brian Lever look like the nastiest bastard."

Two days later Daniel was escorted by security officers into the court room. Four stood behind him as he sat down. To the right sat his parents. He wondered if Brian or any of his former colleagues sat to the left. Woods had advised against looking at Brian's side. He saw Woods and Brooks sit at their table. Hague stood by the public gallery talking to someone. As he walked past he glared at Daniel. He wants to put me away so he can look good to his bosses, and maybe get a fatter bonus, Daniel thought.

"All rise for Judge Abigail Nolan," the clerk ordered.

Daniel looked at the short, dark blonde, stern-faced woman in a black as she walked to her chair. He could see Brian out of the corner of his eye glaring hard at him.

Don't return it, that's what he wants, Daniel told himself.

"Be seated," Nolan said. "This is a plea hearing only. Mr Woods, has your client been made fully aware of the charges against him?"

Woods rose. "Yes your honour he has. I have consulted with him on his options.

"Very well. Stand, Mr Steele."

Daniel got to his feet. "On the charge of ABH how do you wish to plead?"

Daniel took a deep breath. "Not guilty, your honour."

Hague leapt to his feet. "Your honour? How can he plead that? We have the assault on camera, we have witnesses and he even admitted it!"

"Mr Hague!" Nolan snapped. "I will not have that sort of behaviour. Sit down. Perhaps Mr Woods will be good enough to explain."

"Thank you, your honour." Woods stood. "I was going to say we will base this plea on temporary mental instability. We have a psychologist willing to testify to how the store put Mr Steele in a bad state of mind."

"I see." Nolan said. "Is there anything to say to that Mr Hague?"

Hague said. "No, but I do move to have the defendant's bail is revoked,"

Daniel tensed.

"On what grounds?"

"Recently, Mr Lever was harassed and insulted at work by two friends of the defendants. I fear worst will follow."

"Your honour," Woods said. "Whilst my learned friend raises a fair point, he should be aware that Mr Steele was not involved in any way in that incident."

"Can you prove Steele's involvement?" Nolan asked Hague.

"No, but-"

"Then unless there is anything else I will not revoke bail. The same conditions will apply. Do we have anything else?"

No responses came. "Excellent, then I will set the trial to take place in July approximately, at a date to be set by the court."

"Court is adjourned," the clerk announced. "All rise." All present stood and started to walk out.

Rivers stood outside with Lever and Partt. Hague came and joined them.

"Not guilty!" Lever seethed. "What on earth makes him think he can get off?"

"I wouldn't worry," Hague assured him. "It means he will do more time in prison."

"What will they base their plea on?" Partt wondered.

"We've had two store workers come forward since Edmunds was removed," Rivers said.

"Obviously they've been referred to the defence," He looked at Lever.

"The two involved have said you are very unpleasant and insensitive. One is a former worker. A Jack Anson who has Asperger's syndrome has said that you were always putting him down."

"He was a lazy mouthy idiot. Does a man have to defend his right to demand high standards in the work place?" Brian demanded through gritted teeth.

"I'll tear him apart," Hague said.

"These things never existed when I was young. Now these idiots use special needs as an excuse for being slow and incompetent."

"I suggest you calm down. In the court case they will try their best to provoke you." Rivers warned. "And lay off people with special needs."

"Oh are you one of these politically correct types too?" Lever snapped.

"I think I've said enough," Rivers said, walking away.

Hague saw Woods later on.

"You realise you haven't a chance, don't you?" he asked.

"I don't agree?" Woods said calmly.

"Assault is a crime, no matter what the provocation."

"Yes, and so too is victimisation. And prejudice can aggravate the act. Even as recently as a decade ago I would never have had a chance. But now we're a bit more aware of the problems people have, and the prejudice out there. It's not like the Thatcher era where the higher up you were the more things worked in your favour."

"Thatcher was a great lady."

"To people like you and your executive friends; yeah. To people like me, who grew up barely knowing my father because he had to work all the hours to keep us fed; no. People like Daniel Steele would have had no chance. That era went by the rule of 'he who falls behind, gets left behind'."

"I'd agree with that."

Woods glared at him. "Your kind would." He walked away.

Woods had a meeting with Judge Nolan after and then with Dr McLeish. Afterwards he phoned Daniel.

"How are you feeling, Daniel?"

"I've got the jitters bad. Do you still think I did the right thing?"

"I spoke to Dr McLeish. He told me some very interesting things. I can't promise it, but we've a good shot of getting you off. Obviously it depends somewhat on the jury."

"How's that?"

"If we're lucky there'll be some who can relate or at least sympathise. I will have to fight it on legal issues. Hague will do the same I reckon. A court case has to be fought on legal arguments."

EIGHTEEN

Rivers had the day off and decided on a whim to walk into Major's Hardware store to see what he could find out about Daniel Steele's time there. To his relief Miles Booth was not there. He asked a young man if he could speak to the man in charge. A man in his late fifties came forward and Rivers showed him his ID.

"DS Rivers. I need to ask you some questions about Daniel Steele if I could please?"

"Of course, I'm Roger Major. I own this store. You're the one Miles complained about, aren't you?"

"Yes, I'm sorry, I-"

"Don't worry. I know how highly strung Miles is. How can I help?"

"I need to know your opinion on Daniel."

"He was a lovely lad. We were all a bit stunned when we heard about what happened."

"I see. So can you tell me why you dismissed him?"

"He was on his trial period, and he wasn't picking things up fast enough. Don't get me wrong, he was hard working, compliant, and polite. But I need someone who can pick things up quicker, and use a bit more initiative. He used to get aggravated easily too."

"You say he was hard working though?"

"Yes, but after eight weeks when we came to his review period he still couldn't work out where most things in the shop were. When it was busy we couldn't deal with him constantly asking staff where things went and where things were."

"You know he was dyspraxic?"

"He never told me that at the interview."

"Mr Major, he doesn't have to, and if he did would you have employed him?"

"Well, no."

"So why say that?"

Major looked angry. "Look," he said. "This is a business I'm running, not a charity."

"I'm sorry, I meant no offence." Rivers said. Major visibly relaxed.

Major said, "I suggested he should find a job where he just had to do something like sit on a till all day, he could do that."

Rivers stared at the ground. Then looked up. "I'm told Miles told him to stop therapy and learning and just get any job?"

"I really told Miles off for that. I told him he was bang out of order for saying that. It was not his business what Daniel did. Personally I agreed it was a waste of time Daniel doing the courses, but who am I to say?"

"Sorry, what do you mean?"

"Well if he couldn't function in a basic retail job, what hope is there?"

"Maybe he hoped to find his calling elsewhere. Some people find they're not much at one thing, but are in another. Thank you for your time," Rivers said.

Major watched him walk out.

Daniel sat gloomily in The Silver Seal, staring at his pint. Joe and Ricky were with him.

"Ricky, homosexuality is a crime." He heard Joe say in a stupid voice.

"You'll have to give up your hobby then," Ricky grinned. "Or is that like your full time job?"

"Faggot," Joe shot back. "Hey Daniel, what's up?"

"I'm just thinking, what's the point of me even trying to get work? I was at a sandwich bar today, and just looking at the bowls of different ingredients there, I thought I could never work it all out. I can't figure anything. Am I to just work in dead end places all my life for fuck all pay, and bastards like Brian Lever on my case?"

"You could always try back at the supermarket?" Ricky suggested.

"They won't take me back. Remember me saying, Joe, I went for one of the managers the other day?"

"How about you talk to Pete about this?" Joe suggested.

"Why?"

"He thinks highly of you and he's good to talk to about this kind of thing, believe it or not."

Joe got up and went outside.

"You feeling bad about yourself?" Ricky asked.

"Yeah, how about you?"

"I'm fed up of working in the clothes store,"

"So why don't you try something else?"

"Because the one saving grace is the hours. I do the hours I want, and I guess I'm concerned about what could happen out there, you know with the recession always in the news."

"Yeah, I've been put on Jobseekers and every time I have my interview I feel like saying 'all that I see on the news is the recession this and the recession that.' I've had a couple of people say, 'You'll be lucky' when I talk about job searching."

Joe walked back in. "I spoke to Pete. He's out there now, waiting for you." Daniel nodded and went outside.

Pete stood there with some other regulars.

"Come over here," he said, walking away from them.

"Joe said I should talk to you," Daniel said.

"Yeah, what's on your mind? Is it the trial?"

"Among other things. It's about getting a job. I just – just don't have the faith I used to, you know? My last job I finally lost the plot and did something bad.

"Brian's a prick, but I still shouldn't have done it. Fast Service gave me a hard time; the hardware store dismissed me, unofficially of course, because of my problems. I have trouble concentrating because of my angry feelings usually, and then there's the obsessive thoughts."

"What obsessive thoughts?"

"They come and go. They haven't been too bad lately. But they were always making me worry about the lives of people I cared strongly about. Believe me, I know it's bollocks. But it doesn't make them go away."

"Things like that can be bought on by emotional stress. I know what you went through when you were younger. And that's why you're the way you are. Look, you can always call me if you need to talk. The worst that can happen is I'll say I'm too drunk to talk."

Daniel managed a grin.

"As for your work problems, I think if you've got enough in the bank you should go back on the courses you were doing before. Still keep your eyes open for a job, but for one that suits you – not just the first you can get."

"Thanks, Pete," Daniel smiled. "Obviously I couldn't claim JSA for a while because I was dismissed. Just tell me. Do you think I'll go inside?"

"Honestly? It's hard to say. But if you do it'll be a category C prison. But let's hope you get off."

"Thanks again."

"Hey, you're a good 'un. You know Alan will probably be convicted and given a year or so? He's a wrong 'un. He's a liability. You're not."

Rivers sat in the police canteen with DC Sandra Cole.

"I don't think it's good you worrying so much about the Daniel Steele case," she said.

"You ever come across an investigation that brought back bad memories for you?" Rivers asked.

"That's why I do what I do, sarge," Cole said. "My best friend Rian, when I was at school was sexually abused repeatedly from the age of twelve to thirteen by her step-dad. Her alcoholic, depressed mother refused to believe it."

Cole continued, "Rian went off the rails, changed from being a decent ordinary sort, to being into drugs, stealing, vandalism, and then finally got into street mugging. I've not spoken to her since I was twenty. Ten years ago. She hates me for my chosen career. I keep tabs on her. She's been in and out of prison since she was eighteen for mugging, drugs, theft. That's why I don't see things so black and white like Chris Walker does. In some ways I envy him for it."

"I know. It must be easier. Rivers smiled.

"So what does the Steele case bring up for you?"

"Background checks I did on him. He was always picked on and given a hard time because he has special needs, like me," Rivers said.

Sandra looked at him. He continued, "I'm dyspraxic like him. I used to work hard and still get given a hard time. I was told all sorts, about how it was a business, not a charity, I'm not up to the job. I should just work on a till job all my life. Just like Daniel. These bosses, they have such delusions of grandeur about themselves. Roger Major who runs the hardware shop Daniel worked at made it sound like he was in charge of a big corporation. It's just a small shop for fuck sake. I had to put up with people like that. Trying to make out they were more than they were in their employment."

"Are you going to ask to be taken off the case?"

"No. I can't. It's an assault case. Brian Lever is a horrid bastard, but he's the victim in the eyes of the law." Rivers shook his head. "Or is it Daniel Steele, pushed to the edge? Who's the victim?"

NINETEEN

Daniel spent the next two weeks out drinking heavily with friends from The Duke and also with Joe, Ricky and Matt. The two weeks passed in a blur. One night he went in to The Duke to find two of his sister's friends in there. They were called Kevin and Anthony.

"Hey guys," Daniel said. "I'm wrecked."

"That'll be great if the police pull you up," Kevin retorted. "Anyway, shouldn't you be trying to get employed?"

"What's the fucking point? It'll just be repeats of where I was before. Plus all you hear about on the news is about the recession. How do they expect people to keep trying when that's all you hear about?"

"So what?" Kevin demanded. "You're just going to give up are you?"

"No, just take some time out, relax a bit."

"Not being funny, but the trial is approaching, and it won't look good you not working," Anthony put in.

"Forget that," Kevin said angrily. "I had such a high regard for you when I was growing up. You always were an inspiration to people like me."

"So what should I do then?"

"What were you planning to do?"

"As I say, relax for a bit. I don't need a row. Good night gents." He walked away.

The next day Daniel had been to the Job Centre to sign on for JSA. He had had to wait three months before he could start, having been dismissed. He wasn't too worried as he had plenty of money saved from when he was working. But the advisor he spoke to had been harsh.

"Shouldn't have got dismissed should you?" he'd said bluntly.

"What, at a place where I was treated badly and had no life?" Daniel protested.

The advisor had looked at him blankly.

"Is he foreign?" Alan Saunders demanded in The Seal after Daniel told them about it.

"No,"

"Those foreign fucks are taking over and implementing their way," He glared at a black man nearby. "This is our country. If you don't like it, fuck off!"

"Alan," Pete grabbed his arm. "You got a suspended sentence yesterday. We're out celebrating you not being inside. Do you want an anti-climax, to get put inside?"

"Just saying is all," Alan said, becoming docile.

"You can think what you want, just don't shout it," Pete told him.

"Coming for a cigarette, Alan?" Joe asked, opening the back door.

Alan nodded and followed them out.

"Those two, they're so racist it's pathetic," Rees said.

"Just want something to be angry at don't they?" Evan put in.

"Right, never mind those pricks, time to get pissed," Pete put in.

"Whey-heeey," came the response.

The rest of the night passed in a blur of drinking and larking about.

Daniel woke up the next day, not sure where he was. He was on a couch and saw Joe on another.

"Hey Joe, where are we?" he groaned.

Joe woke up. "Steve's place, you know, Alan's mate."

"Oh yeah, I remember now."

Daniel felt dry and pulled himself up to get some water. He staggered into the kitchen and jumped back. A huge swastika was taped to the wall.

When he returned he asked. "Is Steve one of Alan's lot?"

"You see the flag, eh?" Joe chuckled. "Did you not know?"

"Obviously not."

Alan then stumbled in. "What's the old saying? It's not a good night unless you get a traffic cone." He laughed, holding up a hub cap.

"Yeah, that's a hub cap you fucking nob," Joe said.

"So it is. Where'd I get it?"

"You swiped it off Steve's neighbour's car. I hope they don't realise," Daniel grinned.

"So what now, it's eleven in the morning. I'm hung over. Best cure is to get pissed again," Joe said.

"Fair play," Daniel agreed, picking up a half empty beer can and swigging it. Joe nodded and grabbed one. He swigged it and then his eyes bulged, he covered his mouth and ran to throw up in the down stairs toilet.

"He just neck a can of cigarette ash?" Daniel asked.

"Oh yes," Alan laughed. "Stupid bastard."

Joe came back in. "You cunt, Alan, you knew didn't you? Why didn't you say?"

"What? And put you off your drink?" Alan smirked.

When Steve woke up they decided to go to the local C-store to get more beer.

"It's run by a fucking shit skin boys," Steve growled.

"Who cares? We're just getting booze," Daniel laughed.

"I do, our country, and he forced another store to close that had been there since I was nine!" Steve snapped.

They got the drink returned, to Steve's house and relaxed for two hours. Steve and Alan spent a lot of the time being racist.

TWENTY

"Tell me something, Daniel. A decent person like you mixing with louts like that. It makes no sense," Michelle said, as they sat in The Duke that evening.

"Steve and Alan upset the people that run store when we were there. Steve started on at me about the Joe-darkys, that's slang for Pakistanis, being the reason people working in stores get a raw deal."

"That's not true,"

"Sadly, it is. No extra pay for unsocial hours, plus full hours on Sundays and bank holidays. Not the fault of the foreigners, it's a case of these company bosses see a chance for cheap labour and if white born Brits complain they're told to naff off because the boss people know they can hire foreigners to do the job."

"Do you hate them for it?"

"Come on, no. I hate the bastards who take advantage of it. Both them and native born Brits," he sighed.

"The point I need to make is that earlier I was in The Eagles Nest where I was talking to my friend Andy who I worked with at the hardware store, about this. He asked why I hang around with these people. I told him it's because with them I fit in. They understand me better than people round here do. I feel more at ease with them. When I'm with my lot from the supermarket they don't get my issues, same as the lot here, or even if they do they make out like they don't, and now most of them stick their noses up at me because of what I did. When I'm with the lot from the Seal I don't get judged, or made to feel inferior."

"I don't know what to say to that."

"There's nothing to say, but you'll be glad to hear I've gone back into therapy. Got an appointment Tuesday week, with a different doctor obviously."

"Why not the previous one?"

"He's speaking on my behalf in the trial." He smiled uneasily. "Part of me dreads it approaching. The other wants it over."

Michelle smiled then looked up. "Hi Kyle," she said.

Kyle Lennard was Daniel's age, tall and well-built, but with a large gut from no exercise. He was not well thought of by most of The Dukes regulars, who found him arrogant and patronizing. Michelle however had a very high opinion of him.

"It's been a while," Daniel said.

"Yeah, haven't seen you since before you got arrested. Aren't you ashamed of yourself?" Kyle demanded.

Daniel was taken aback. "It was wrong, but this man picked on me all the time."

"Oh Danny, you forget, I was a supervisor at the supermarket and I would have been on your case if we'd been on the same section in the supermarket when I worked with you."

"Why would you?"

"Because, young Danny, you didn't pick things up like you should have. You were just great entertainment to some of us."

"Yeah, you and Sean Mortimer. You were useless yourself, we all used to laugh at you behind your back for thinking you were so great."

"At least I never bashed up old men."

"I thought we were friends."

"Well, you disgust me. Beating a man for expecting high standards."

"Can we please stop this?" Michelle said firmly.

"Look, we'll meet next Tuesday, I'll let you know how my session went," Daniel smiled at her and got up to walk away.

"Yeah, piss off, go to prison you thug," Kyle yelled.

Daniel gritted his teeth and went inside. People turned to look at him. People who he had considered his friends.

A week later in The Silver Seal Daniel was with Joe, Ricky, Evan and Pete. Pete and Evan were talking about work. Both had been temporarily laid off.

"A good kebab lunch there," Ricky said.

"Yeah, when are we going to your place next?" Joe asked.

"My parents go away in five weeks. Just remember to behave."

"Oh yeah, they didn't see the funny side to the boxer shorts in their bed. Did they think you had your male lover over again?"

"Joe, keep your fantasies to yourself," Ricky shot back.

"Can't you two slags stop bitching?" Pete suddenly asked.

"Go back to talking about tossing off your builder mates," Joe replied.

Pete sighed and went over to Joe. He held Joe's wrist and slammed his hand against the radiator.

"Ahh, Pete, no!" Joe gasped.

"Pete, that's enough," Daniel said.

Pete let Joe's wrist go and looked surprised. "That's enough? He hasn't stopped winding me up for the last two hours."

Pete turned back to Evan and they started talking again.

"That burned." Joe shook his hand. "Hey, Daniel, what's been up with you today?"

"Thinking about people in The Duke. Lot of them think badly of me."

"Fuck them, ignorant bastards!" Joe said angrily.

"You think? I attacked an old man. Nasty bastard or not, they'll never look at me the same."

He looked forward. "I'd be the same in their position. The guy is fifty-seven. I just lost it for a few seconds. I mean I have violent urges more and more since I started there. That Miles Booth for one, he was like Brian. I'd approach to ask him where something was and it'd be, 'sigh, what can't you find now, Daniel?' I thought about his kind more and more. At the supermarket it was the same. My confidence meant I won over a lot of people but my dyspraxia problems made a fair few think bad of me."

"I've had people with special needs work for me," Pete put in. "Don't get me wrong, I've had a couple that used it to blame for laziness, but the rest all worked hard, it took them longer to get there, sure. But the effort was there. Was that Lever bloke picking on you for that?"

"Not in his eyes. He just saw me as stupid and lazy. After the first eight weeks when I realised things would not change, despite the assurances that they would by the manager who interviewed me, my work ethic dropped."

"The shifts they had you doing? I'm not surprised," Evan said.

Pete put his hand up. Behind him Daniel heard two well-spoken young men.

"By the time I get to twenty-eight I could be a director. Hard work is what it's about, Darren."

"Too right. There's a recession on and these unemployed people out there use it as an excuse not to work. There are still plenty of jobs out there."

"I feel the same way. The people who don't have much going for them should just accept what they get. I mean, you only live once."

"Talk about a king telling a beggar to make the most of their meal," Daniel muttered.

"I mean, those unemployed should have to do community service until they start work again," one continued.

"I agree. Treat them like the criminals they are."

"Can you believe the arrogance of these two?" Pete muttered.

"Daddy probably bought that one his job," Evan growled.

"Hey," Pete said loudly to the two young men. "Those kind of views are not welcome in here. Either a change of topic or location is in order."

The smaller of the two nodded, but the second one, taller and strongly built retorted, "It's a free country. I can say what I like."

"What I mean is there are people here with these problems that might be offended by that sort of talk. I'm doing you a favour," Pete said back.

"Well that's their problem. So you mind your business, and I'll mind mine," the bigger one said.

"Pete, don't," Evan tried, but, Pete brushed past him and moved closer.

"Just fuck off now! I've asked you nicely, now I'm telling you."

"Hey, Ross, we don't want trouble," the other one said futilely.

"If you want me to leave then make me," Ross said.

"This is your last warning," Pete said calmly. "Change of topic, or location."

"You lot are probably the types who take benefits aren't you? My taxes pay for you to do fuck all!" Ross snapped.

Pete then lurched forward. Ross brought his right arm up to push Pete back but Pete grabbed him by the wrist with his right hand and by the elbow with the left. He twisted his arm to the side, then spun him around, kicked the back of his knees so Ross went down Pete caught him, pulled his right arm behind his back and marched him to the door and threw him outside.

Evan approached the other one. "Sorry that had to happen," he said, gently. "But your mate should have wound his neck in."

"I'll – I'll go now," the other man, Darren said nervously and ran out.

"What an arrogant bastard," Pete growled, walking back over.

"I reckon his type's a snitch. We'd better take a swerve," Daniel said.

"Fuck it. Let him!" Pete snarled.

"They're looking for any excuse to bang me up," Daniel said.

"Fair point," Pete agreed. "Let's go."

TWENTY-ONE

"Morning, sarge," Walker called out to Rivers.

"Morning to you, Chris. What's up?"

"We had a Ross Grant make a complaint of being physically ejected from The Silver Seal last night, for speaking his mind," Walker told him.

"Meaning what?"

"Sarge, it's irrelevant. If you must know it was because he had said there was no excuse to be unemployed and Pete Redmond threw him out for it." Walker sighed.

"Was Daniel Steele there?" Rivers asked.

"I showed him a picture of Steele. Yeah, he was."

"Did he do anything?" Rivers wanted to know.

"I guess you could call him an accessory as he was there and did nothing about it." Walker suggested.

"Oh come on! Pete Redmond has a psychotic temperament. Can you really say if you weren't a police officer you'd get in his way?"

"We arrested Redmond last night. But he was released at nine without charge – for now anyway. The point is, sarge, how long before they think it might be clever to intimidate or harass Brian Lever again?"

"So what's your point?"

"Find some way to lock up Steele as a message. For all we know one of those hot heads might kill Brian Lever out of principle."

Rivers smiled. "You know as well as I do we can't revoke his bail like that. We can't blame him for what Redmond did. Pete Redmond has been charged three times in the last two years for assault and never been convicted. The reason being he is the one provoked." Walker looked stunned. "I've checked, all three occasions he was started on by someone else, he warned them, and then beat them to the ground, but not enough to warrant CPS being prepared to go the full mile. And not many of us have any sympathy for these types who pick a fight, lose and then go whining about it."

"Reasonable force -"

"Was put in by people sitting in cosy offices. When I was twenty-two I saw a yob go for someone. The man he went for put him down and kicked him unconscious. Know why? Because he was scared of what he might do if he got up."

"I still think they're all a threat, Steele's lot I mean."

"If you'd feel better I'll go have a talk with Mr Steele later, OK?"

Walker nodded.

Rivers decided to do it after his shift. He went to the supermarket. Walking up to the Meat and Fish counter he saw the two teenage men on it arguing.

"Harry, this is the tenth time you've had to be told how to fillet plaice. How thick are you?"

"Look, I'm trying hard, but I just have trouble understanding."

"No wonder some of the customers hate you."

"But I'm polite."

"Yes, but useless. You still can't cut steak properly. Management would love to get rid of you, but they know as I do, you'd just go blaming it on prejudice against your special needs."

"I just -"

"Shut it, or you'll get a thump!"

"Excuse me." Rivers went to be served by the bully.

"Yes sir, what can I get you?" The bully now smiled, friendly.

"I'll have half a pound of fantail prawns, and be quick about it!"

The bully carried the request out and Rivers winked at Harry who smiled uneasily back.

"Two hundred and twenty grams," the bully said weighing them.

Rivers sighed. "Are you so thick you don't understand what half a pound is?"

"It's five grams off," the bully shifted nervously.

"Fine, price it up."

"Yes, sir. I'm sorry. It's just frustrations of my day."

"Really?" Rivers took the bag. "The next time I see you picking on someone, mate. I'll be waiting for you outside, and I'll show you what bullying really is. Maybe if you weren't making him so nervous he wouldn't make mistakes so much." The bully's face fell. Rivers smiled and walked away.

Walker and Spears went to The Silver Seal at about eight that evening.

"I thought DS Rivers was going to talk to Steele," Spears said.

"Can I tell you something in confidence Craig? I don't trust Mike at the moment. I think he's getting a bit personally involved here. That's why I said I'd check here and he could check The Duke. Steele is more likely to be here than there."

"Can't you see the sarge's point of view on this Chris? I mean he's practically looking at a mirror image of himself at that age."

"Mistreated or not it's irrelevant to me. Steele attacked a man. Do you think he could or should get off?"

"It may come to the fact that he was denied therapy because his manager found it inconvenient. Not being funny, Chris, but Fast Service have a pretty bad record of treating their employees. The workers get paid peanuts, while the directors earn tonnes. They use intimidation to get results."

"That's business I'm afraid," Walker chuckled. "I don't see him, but I see Redmond." They strode over. Pete rolled his eyes.

"Here to arrest me?" he asked.

"If only," Walker said. "Where's Daniel?"

"You've got to understand that nine times out of ten none of this is arranged. Whoever is here is here. Only Joe and Evan are around, and that's it."

"So you don't know where he is?" Walker asked. Pete shook his head. "You sure? Because if you're lying I could have you for obstructing an investigation."

"Bollocks. If he's done nothing wrong – at present then no you can't. Come on, I'm not some naïve street lout."

"I want to know something," Spears said. "Did any of you encourage him to attack Brian Lever?"

"Let me be honest with you," Pete said. "In the building trade you get a lot of layabout types who you have to be tough with, especially for the wage they're on, which is a good one. But Daniel was on little more than minimum wage and being expected to be top notch by some prick with a fat company pension. He worked for me briefly, Daniel did. He was a grafter. But use and abuse people, they sometimes say 'fuck you' and lose their motivation."

"Do you think it made it right what he did?" Walker asked.

"Would it surprise you if I said no? I know I've a record but I discourage fighting."

"You still do it," Spears said.

"I've got a temper and I know it, but at least I can say it's not me who starts it. What about all these street thugs who batter people for no reason? I remember Shane behind the bar got battered by a gang of teen thugs last year, what did you lot do? Slapped their wrists and said 'don't do it again'. And now you want to put Daniel inside because he lashed out at a bully."

"It comes down to the CPS and the judges; not us. I hate it too when these bastards walk away from it," Spears growled.

Rivers walked into The Duke. He looked around inside, no sign. He saw a back door and went out it. He saw Daniel sitting with a blonde woman who looked in her early thirties.

"Daniel," he said.

Daniel looked up. "Can't you leave me in peace? I've done nothing."

Rivers placed his wallet, phone and keys on the table. He emptied out his pockets. "This is unofficial Daniel. See, no warrant card. I just want to talk ."

"So talk." Daniel shrugged.

"Alone."

"I want Michelle here." He nodded at the woman.

"All right," Rivers sat down. "Daniel, I'm supposed to talk about the case, I'm supposed to have a tape recorder in my pocket." He smiled. "It's in my jacket which I left in my car. But I came to talk about you."

Daniel sipped his beer. "I don't follow you."

"I'm not the enemy, Daniel, not tonight. Know what I saw today when I was shopping? A person with learning difficulties being sadistically bullied, just like I used to be. I worked in a few jobs and almost every time I was made to feel like I should just sit back and do nothing, and then a boss would bollock me for not doing much. Is that how it was for you?"

"Sort of. I was quite mild mannered up until about three years ago when I realised that just sitting back and taking it just got you treated bad. Then I started back-chatting because at the supermarket I found some of the people automatically blamed me for anything going wrong. The section manager told me I had an attitude. I smiled and said 'at least people respect me for it'."

"I know about the time you got attacked as well."

"Yeah, bastards collared me, took me someplace quiet. For half an hour I was begging and crying for them not to kill me. They made me think I was going to be killed, but just slashed me up instead."

"They got three years didn't they?"

"Yeah. Being under eighteen and pleading guilty got them reduced sentences for GBH. The leader, Lewis Cox got five and a half because he was eighteen. The threats were discounted. My word against theirs. That screwed me up a bit. Michelle here has been really supportive."

"I was badly bullied at school for being thick, but I wasn't, I was just made to feel it, so at twelve I stopped trying. Left school with only four D-F grade GCSEs. I consider myself lucky I got them. I went to college thinking there'd be more maturity. I did a low grade GNVQ, got picked on for the same reasons. I was small built too."

"You what? You aren't now."

"No, when I was nineteen I started doing a few hours weight training a week, then after I recovered from my nervous breakdown when I was twenty-five, I really got into it. Started ten to twelve hours a week on average for a year, and then just fell back to four."

"You had a breakdown?" Michelle asked suddenly.

"When I was twenty-three. I just gave up. I was sectioned briefly. Came out, under psychiatric treatment for a year. Then at twenty-seven I joined the police. Found my calling you could say. Now at thirty-five I'm a detective-sergeant,"

"What caused your breakdown?" Michelle asked.

"At school, at college and at work I was put down, made to feel worthless. A lot of dyspraxics have trouble socially. I just gave up as it were." He smiled. "By the way I met your employer at Major Hardware. What an ignorant bastard."

Daniel smiled.

"Roger Major isn't a bad person, he just likes the easy life too much. It was too much hassle in his eyes to train me and take longer. He likes to spend two hours down the pub, and spends most the time at work chatting to people in the store, but it's his business, his prerogative. But I don't feel at £5.98 an hour that I was paid then, he's got any right to give it large about how it's not a charity, it's a business.

"He lost his rag with me, a week after giving me the four week dismissal notice and he had the right to. He'd sent me home the previous day because I'd injured my leg in karate training.

"I freaked out that it would not get better and OD'ed on the diazepam I was on at the time. So I was as high as a kite at work that day.

"Roger said decent enough, that with my limping I should go home. So I did. Next day he had a right go. That was fair enough, but then after I apologised about the third or fourth time and he kept going on, and saying how he had to come in on his day off because of me being so unreliable, and he was being quite offensive, I got the impression he wanted to provoke me so he could sack me on the spot."

"And then there's Miles Booth," Rivers smiled.

"The most racist, prejudice, judgemental person I've ever met," Daniel smiled, clearly relaxed now. "He's your age, Mr Rivers and lives at home, fair enough, but has no social life or ambitions. He wouldn't last long without his parents or his cushy job."

"Do you think he takes it out on anyone he considers more inadequate than him?" Rivers asked.

"In his eyes, no. I think that subconsciously that's the case. He certainly had no patience. Was always snapping 'what can't you find now Daniel' at me, same as Brian Lever did."

"We're not talking about Brian Lever, OK," Rivers said curtly.

"Sorry, but Miles was always on my case when I struggled. Told me to give up on my courses and get any job. In my fragile state, I did. Before that when I went in to see my friend Andy there, I'd be polite and say 'See you' to Miles. He would practically snap, 'See you, Daniel' at me."

"What makes people like him think they've got the right to be so judgemental?" Michelle wondered aloud.

"The other issue are your friends in The Silver Seal,"

"What about them?"

"Come on, Daniel. How many times have they been in trouble? Matt Tyrell and Ricky Ball are the only ones who've never been in grief."

"I thought this chat was more about dyspraxic problems?"

"I'm just saying. Can't you persuade him, Michelle?"

"The thing is, is they're there for him," Michelle said. "I don't approve of them, but they look after him."

"Right," Daniel agreed. "Look, my lot who I knew from the supermarket who were once good friends have virtually disowned me since I stopped working there. My birthday party last year, they all cancelled on me bar two, and they never understood me.

"Turned out one of them got worked up about me having mental health problems and they ditched me because they didn't understand. Except Michelle here the lot here don't understand me. The guys at the Seal do. I know some have got previous, I realise trouble is connected with them, but they're the ones I can depend on."

"You should stop being around them so much," Rivers told him.

"And then do what? They're the only ones who seem to look out for me. I need a slash and a refill."

He shook his empty pint. "Back in a bit." He walked away.

"You see I think one of them goaded Daniel into it," Rivers said.

Michelle shook her head. "You'd be wrong," She looked sadly at him. "I did."

Rivers looked stunned. "I beg your pardon?"

"It wasn't the way you think, please hear me out. Daniel is a very compassionate person."

"Dyspraxic people usually are," Rivers said.

Michelle forced herself to speak. "When I had married my husband we lived in West Heyford. In my regular pub there I met this one bloke called Dave Durrant. He posed as a friend then I met two other friends of his. They joked playfully, or so I thought about having a gang bang. Then one night, walking home–" she breathed deeply.

"I got stopped by Dave. He said it was time for fun. His friends appeared. I asked what they meant. He flashed at me, and smirking said 'You know, you gave us all the call signs'. Then one grabbed me, one taped my mouth and-"

Rivers reached out. "I can guess the rest. They gang raped you, yes?"

She nodded, her eyes moist.

"You talked to Daniel, the night before didn't you? One witness said he'd snapped about how there were worse things in this world. Look, come see me at the station and we'll talk, off the record about things."

"That'd be good," she said, choking back emotions. "In his state of mind it pushed him too far. I feel partly responsible."

"I see, now go to the toilet and fix yourself up. I think I've said all I have to say." He dug in his pocket. "Here's my card. Call me and we'll fix an appointment." Michelle took it and walked away. Rivers went inside and put on his jacket. He saw Daniel at the bar talking to someone.

"I was about to come outside," he said.

"Forget it. I've said all I have to." Rivers leaned closer. "Remember, I'm the enemy again in the morning. You claim to anyone this conversation took place, I'll deny it. Understand?" Daniel nodded. "We understand each other then."

TWENTY-TWO

Two days later, Rivers stared at his computer screen. Cole was next to him.

"So Burroughs gave you a real chewing out over the talk with Daniel Steele?" Cole asked.

Rivers grinned wryly. "Yeah, shit recorder clicked off. He didn't say anything of interest though. But Burroughs thinks I'm just covering, and I can't prove different. What does interest me though is Daniel's friend I met, Michelle Fielder. No previous on her, but she says she was gang raped. The leader she says was a Dave Durrant. I've looked this man up. Not a nice guy, but he was found not guilty of raping her."

"Where is he now?"

"Two years ago he was sentenced to ten years for attempted murder. He glassed some bloke and then tried to stab them too. He'd previously done time twice for ABH and theft. But was found not guilty of rape."

"Rape's hard to prove. Doesn't mean he was innocent."

"I'd agree."

"Sarge." Walker came in. "A young woman to see you, regarding Steele."

"Excellent," Rivers clicked out of the screen. He got up.

Walker followed him into the corridor.

"Who is she?"

"My visit to The Duke wasn't all in vain. She interests me, this one. She wants to speak for Steele."

"Should I sit in?"

"No, I think she'll only speak to me in full."

"Sarge, it feels like you're shutting me out here. I don't appreciate it."

"Don't take it personally. Would you want me in on a snitch that trusts you?" Rivers hesitated. "Oh alright, I have to have another officer present. Just stay silent and let me do the talking."

Rivers met Michelle by the entrance with Walker.

"Good morning," Rivers smiled. "Do you want to come with me?"

She nodded and followed him to an interview room. Rivers ushered her in and she sat. He explained about Walker sitting in as procedure.

"Michelle, do you want this unofficial? I can record the interview. But it could swing for or against Daniel."

"Record it," she said, quickly.

"All right," Rivers switched it on. "Interview taking place, February the nineteenth, thirteen forty-four. Present is Detective Sergeant Rivers..."

"And DC Walker." Walker said.

"And Michelle Fielder, speaking on behalf of Daniel Steele. Please state your name for the benefit of the tape." Rivers said.

"Michelle Fielder."

"Thank you. Now, Michelle we met two nights ago at The Duke in Mansford, correct?"

"Yes."

"Now you told me about when you were sexually assaulted eight years ago. You should understand I have checked and found that the men in question, David Durrant, Jason Ferdinand and Calum Atkins were all found not guilty."

"They did it!" she gasped. "They claimed I consented to doing it in an empty field with tape to my mouth for erotic excitement. None of them broke on the witness stand and their defence made out I lied to cover my back against my husband who did believe me, but my parents didn't and claimed I had disgraced them. They haven't spoken to me in seven years since the trial."

"All right. At issue here is that you say this pushed Daniel Steele over the edge and led to him assaulting a Brian Lever. How is this so?"

"Daniel's known it for as long as we've known each other almost. He'd told me what had happened to him. The night before I'd talked about the effects of what I went through has had on me. The look on his face was of pure rage. He was talking evenly to me, but I could actually feel the anger, do you know what I mean?"

"I suppose so." Rivers said.

"Later another young man came in. He's the one who helped me through a suicidal phase before I knew Daniel. There's some tension between this man and Daniel."

"His name please?" Rivers asked, pleased that Walker was staying silent.

"Kyle Lennard. He started winding Daniel up about his inadequacies in the work place. Daniel looked like he was going to attack him. So I led him away and asked Kyle to leave us when he tried to follow."

"Was he trying to actually provoke a fight from Daniel?"

"No. Me and Kyle are very close friends. Trying to calm Daniel down I could feel the pure anger in him. He said to me it just summed up all his problems."

"Would he have gone for Kyle Lennard if you had not have been there?"

"I don't know, just that I wasn't prepared to risk it."

"So you think all the emotions from that night may have pushed him over the edge?"

"Yes. Being denied therapy. The shifts he was doing, lack of a social life. He was getting more and more volatile. But it's a business's prerogative to do that isn't it?"

"Yes, except denying therapy. Is there anything else?"

"No."

"Interview terminated, thirteen forty-seven." Rivers switched off the recorder. "Is there anything you'd like to tell me now?"

She nodded. "It's just, that Daniel's always looking at me like I can make it all right for him. There are times when I go to talk to other people and he seems to get offended by it. He tags on to me sometimes. He and Kyle seem to have this competitiveness in them for my attention."

"Who are you closer to?"

"Kyle. The attachment was formed by him helping me out at a very bad time I went through emotionally three years ago,"

"What do other people make of them?"

"A lot of people dislike Daniel since the incident. His name wasn't mentioned in the paper, but it's common knowledge. People dislike Kyle too, they think he's arrogant and condescending, but he's not."

"I'm sorry to say this Michelle, but some people change their personalities to suit who they're with. Look, I can refer this to Daniel's defence and you can appear as a character witness for him. Just be aware that the prosecutor is a brutally ruthless man, who will use the trial you went through to the full."

"I'll still do it. Can you advise me on how to deal with the prosecutor?"

"Me, no. The defence will. They'll meet you before you speak."

"Thanks. Can I go now?"

"I just want to know, do you see those men who attacked you? Not Durrant obviously. He's doing life."

"That's why me and Ruari, my husband moved here, to escape them. A year later I read in the local paper that Jason Ferdinand died as a result of a drug overdose and Calum Atkins who also was more a follower moved away shortly after. Would it be a terrible thing to say that I'm glad the two main perpetrators got their comeuppance?"

Rivers smiled. "No, it wouldn't. I'll lead you out."

Rivers phoned Woods later.

"I've got another character witness for you. That makes five doesn't it?... Yeah, so that's three from Fast Service, one a former employee, this lady and Joe McGinty.

"Is Joe McGinty really a good idea? He's an unemployed boozer is why... All right, your decision. I'll let you have the taped interview when you next come in. Let me know. Yeah, yeah." He hung up.

"Sarge," Walker said. "The DI wants to see you," He looked grim.

"What am I supposed to have done this time?"

"I don't want to say."

"All right" Rivers got up and walked to the office. He knocked on the door and went in. "You wanted to see me ma'am."

"Yes, close the door, Michael," Burroughs said. Rivers complied and stood in front of the desk. She stood facing him, "You should know DS Rivers I have decided to take you off the Daniel Steele case. However Superintendent Palmer has ruled in your favour."

"Why would you have done that?"

Burroughs glared at him. "How many complaints have I had about you since January the eleventh when this all started?

"I realise you're dealing with issues relevant to yourself, but we can't let that affect our judgement. You have taken all of this very personally, and I believe you not only deliberately cocked up the talk with Steele the other night, but that you hope he will get off. Now I dare you to lie to me!" She shouted the last sentence.

"I want him found guilty ma'am, but I don't want to see him going to prison. Assault is a crime, but so too is victimisation."

Burroughs thumped her right fist on the desk making Rivers jump. "Brian Lever has never been convicted or put on trial for that. I also know you spoke to a woman earlier who accused three men of rape once."

"She is adamant that they did it."

"I don't believe I'm hearing this. The three men were found not guilty, therefore they were innocent."

"Only because the jury thought so, it doesn't mean they were."

"Back to the Daniel Steele investigation, the superintendent says to keep you on in spite of all this and whilst I disagree with him I must bow to his decision. In that I will have to trust you – sadly. Is this clear?"

"Yes, ma'am."

"Now get out!" she snapped, pointing to the door.

Rivers got as far as four steps out of Burroughs office before he heard his name called again. He turned to see Palmer there.

"Michael, I want to see you in half an hour," Palmer said.

"Are you going to have a go at me as well sir?"

"As I said, in half an hour," Palmer said firmly. He walked out.

DS Warren Hampson whistled. "Not good for you, Mikey is it," he sneered.

Rivers and Hampson openly despised one another. Hampson had only got where he was by screwing over some former colleagues who had used excessive baton force on a repeat offender of domestic violence. Hampson also had a problem with Rivers because he knew his past.

"Get fucked Warren," Rivers muttered.

"Naughty boy, you. Sticking up for retards and liars." Hampson smirked.

"What?"

"Just what I heard the guv talking to Chris about how you took a statement off a woman who lied about being raped. And how you feel sorry for one of your retarded brothers that you're actually meant to be prosecuting," Hampson chuckled.

Then he said calmly. "By the way, Mike, how are your learning problems coming on? How did you ever get this job anyway?"

"By hard graft, I didn't snitch on my friends like you did."

"I guess you feel sorry for that bloke who hit his boss. The one with problems, probably reminds him of you eh?" Hampson grinned nastily.

Rivers turned and stared at him. Suddenly, he lunged in Hampson's direction. Walker and DC Gavin Webb got in between them and restrained Rivers.

"Arrogant fucker, it's because of your kind that people like him and me go the way we are!"

"Let it go, this is what he wants!" Walker snapped.

"I'm just stating some facts is all," Hampson stared back down at his reports looking unfazed.

"Just let it go," Webb said.

Burroughs charged out.

"What's all this?" she demanded.

"Disagreement got out of hand," Webb tried.

"As you can see ma'am, Sergeant Rivers tried to go for me," Hampson said.

"You're in enough trouble today as it is Rivers, go to Palmer's office – now!" Burroughs thundered.

"I was going to see him anyway," Rivers muttered, and walked away.

When Rivers reached the office Palmer was waiting for him.

"Sit down, Mike," he said. Rivers complied. "Did you just go for DS Hampson?"

"Yeah, I don't think I'd have attacked him if I'd have got there though."

"Look, he doesn't win popularity contests, that one. I'd be hard pressed to find five people at this station who actually trust him. But you realise that this, plus the number of complaints I've had, I can't let this go. I'm going to have to advise you to take a weeks leave."

"Sir, I realise that's what you have to do."

"Good. Now what I originally asked to speak to you about was the conversation myself and DI Burroughs had earlier."

"What is going on, Mike? You're one of the most effective people in CID and you know that. Do you realise how bad I will be made to look if you mess up on this case? Now I need you to tell me. What is going through your head?"

"Sometimes, sir, we wonder who the real victim is, you know?"

"Yes, I had to put a woman away when I was a DC for killing her violent husband. It tore me up, but I had to do it. I was lucky though. She got off light under self-defence because her defence made it clear he would have killed her. Long story, there was a lot more to it than that."

"You see Daniel Steele seems to be going through what I used to. When I look at him, I see myself. I see an alternative version of myself. I used to think of thumping victimising colleagues, but I never had it in me."

"You empathise with his plight?" Palmer asked, and Rivers nodded. "I need you to be truthful with me. Can I rely on you to do the right thing when you return? Can I rely on you, during your time off, not to conduct your own private investigation?"

Rivers swallowed hard. "Yes, sir. You can. I've plenty of cash saved. I'll go away for a few days."

"Good man. See to it you do. I have to say this though Mike. If you do violate the conditions that myself and DI Burroughs have set, you'll be up for disciplinary. I'd hate to see a police officer of your excellent record up for that."

"Yes, sir."

"Good, now collect your things and go.

If DS Hampson tries to provoke you, ignore him."

"Yes sir," Rivers turned and left.

TWENTY-THREE

Daniel sat in The Anchor, one of Mansford's quieter pubs, on his own, nursing a pint. It was just after five in the afternoon. Only a few others were there. He did not see the two come in.

"Well, look here, Stuart, if it isn't the local delinquent," Kyle smirked at Stuart Berry.

"Sitting here like a loser on his own," Berry sneered.

"It's common knowledge what you did you know," Kyle sneered. "Nobody thinks you're a hero for it. Bashing an old man up." Stuart sat down and started toying with a piece of loose wood.

"You know, even if you walk, you'll never live it down. Just like the plastic chorizo incident." Kyle sniggered.

"How many people want to know you from the supermarket, eh? No one. Just like The Duke. A couple of people have asked for you to be banned."

"They can go screw a dog," Daniel muttered.

"That's not nice," Kyle replied. "It's nice of Michelle to want to speak for you, but, the prosecutor will bring up things she tries to forget. Shows how selfish you are."

Daniel sipped his pint and ignored them.

"You're just a sad failure aren't you?" Stuart chuckled.

"We knew it. Now everyone knows it."

Daniel breathed deeply.

Kyle looked around. "Hey, everyone. This is the guy who bashed up the old boy in the Fast Service store," he shouted. People looked over.

"Was that, Brian?" A middle aged woman asked. "He's a good fellow. I talk to him Thursday mornings when I go in there."

The landlord, a short squat man with red hair and a moustache looked sternly from behind the bar at Daniel. "Your kind aren't welcome here. Out now!"

"Better do as he says," Stuart smirked.

"This is not right!" Daniel cried out.

"Got a problem with it? Call the old bill," The landlord grunted. "Out – now! Or I'll call them."

"Yes, you don't need that, what with the trial approaching," Kyle said nastily.

Daniel faced him. "You were incompetent too. You just thought you were really good. Did your leaving do that only three people came to not tell you how popular you were?"

Daniel swigged his pint and forced himself to ignore shoves from Stuart and Kyle.

"I hope they bang you up!" The middle aged woman shouted after him.

Daniel stormed a long the empty streets. He dug his phone out and called Michelle.

"Daniel, I'm busy cooking the kids' dinner," she answered.

"Just one thing Michelle," he sighed. "Kyle, he's a fucking cunt! I wish his dad had bashed him about more when he was a kid!"

"That's a terrible thing to say," she gasped.

"So is what he just did. He's going around telling people what I did. It's only because he helped you out I don't let my lot from the Seal batter him!"

"Now you're talking stupidly. I don't want to hear this."

"No, because he's so great to you? Why do you think most people in The Duke hate him?"

"If you want me to speak for you in court I suggest you hang up now. I'm very tempted to refuse anyway," she told him.

Daniel clicked off. "Ignorant,-" he started then stopped. He went to sit on a bench to calm down.

That night he met Joe in The Silver Seal, Rees, Pete and Matt were there to.

"Can you believe what happened to Daniel guys?" Joe snapped. "These two fuckers gave him grief and have turned people against him."

"You should go to the police. That's harassment," Matt said.

"They won't fucking care," Pete said. "To them he deserves what he gets."

"Well, let's do those bastards over then," Joe snapped.

"Chances are we all get done in then," Rees commented. "People like that are best ignored. It's hard, I know. I used to get it in the neck after I came out from being inside. But you have to grit your teeth and ignore it."

"We could make it out to be a street fight that got out of hand!" Joe suggested.

"Yeah, and then what?" Pete demanded. "They catch us and link us to Daniel. They'll find a way to implicate him and inside he goes. Like Rees says you have to grit your teeth and bear it. Just remember, Daniel, to that 'normal' lot you're being done in for an assault you committed so don't expect any sympathy."

"So what? We just let it slide?" Joe snapped.

"There's no other choice," Matt said. "Do you think we want that? No, but there's nothing we can do."

"How many weeks away is the trial, Daniel?" Pete asked.

"Seven," Daniel said. "I've had a letter."

"Now you haven't tried too hard to find a new job have you?" Pete said.

"No point is there? With what I did and all I see on the news about the recession."

"But you're on Jobseekers. That will not look good. I remember you saying to me about that young bloke who said you should do something else. I agree. Go back to Train to Gain. Start your course again and see if your new psychologist can get you on to Incapacity benefit."

"What so I'm under no obligation to find work?"

"Yes. That and you'll get shifted to the lot who help people out with difficulties getting work. Trust me here. Both will help make you look good, even if you're found guilty."

Later that night though when Joe, Daniel and Matt had gone to Joe's house Pete was alone with Rees.

"Daniel's going to be found guilty isn't he?" Pete growled.

Rees nodded. "I'd say so. Nothing we can do."

"You're wrong there." Pete looked around to make sure no one was looking and then flashed his work knife quickly.

"What are you thinking Pete?" Rees asked.

"I'm going to get that cunt who's pressing charges, hold it to his throat and tell him he's a dead man if he doesn't drop the charges."

"Pete, no. That man will just snitch, and then Daniel will get blamed."

"Not if I scare him. Can you see Daniel surviving in prison Rees? All this because some old bastard gives him a hard time about having special needs."

"Listen, Pete. We've known each other since being inside. You know as well as I do, they'll put that man into protective custody, bang you up, and bang Daniel up. These young men look up to us, even though you're a right bastard to Joe and Matt sometimes." Both men smiled. "It's all about pointing them in the right direction and then sticking to it."

Daniel held the letter in his hands that he had received a few days ago. The court summons. Telling him about the trial. 8th July until the 12th. He knew that he had five character witnesses to speak for him; Jimmy Hatton and Wayne Isaacs. Wayne a former worker there. Joe and Michelle as long as he didn't upset her again.

Also Jack Anson, another former worker at Fast Service. He started to think. Jimmy might be all right against the prosecutor, and Wayne, but Jack had been in a lot of trouble at work for attitude. Joe would be torn apart for being unemployed and Michelle for having had three men charged who had then walked. Part of him did feel selfish for asking her do it.

There was no saying how many witnesses the prosecution would bring against him. A young karate fighter attacked a man who was almost an OAP. No jury would find him innocent?

Daniel walked into the Silver Seal. He saw Joe and Matt at the bar.

"I'm going to change my plea," Daniel blurted out.

"What?" They both gasped.

"I'm going to call up my lawyer and change my plea to guilty,"

"Why would you do that?" Matt gasped.

"I can't win. The evidence is overwhelming."

"You stupid fucking idiot!" Joe snapped. "Don't even think about it. Trust me; They want you to freak out. You're going to have doubts. It's normal, OK."

"I'm going to be found guilty,"

"Are you guilty in your opinion?" Joe asked.

"No."

"Then don't talk shit."

"Listen, I'll give you a more intelligent argument than Joe has." Matt smiled.

"You arsehole." Joe grinned back.

"Forget your idiot character witnesses," Matt continued.

"Hey, I'm one," Joe said.

"Exactly," Matt said. "If your doctor can persuade the jury that you were not mentally, well, you will be found innocent. Not to mention the bloke you hit was a bully anyway. If it can be proved, you'll be found innocent. Unless you get-"

"I'd stop there Matt," Daniel smiled.

"Matt can't help it. He's ethnically challenged, the black bastard," Joe smirked.

"This black bastard's doing a lot better than you ever will, and earning more," Matt shot back.

"What a group we've got," Joe sighed. "One cocoa chunter." He nodded at Matt. "Ricky who I reckon is as straight as a zigzag. Daniel the bastard with a receding hairline, Pete the psycho, Evan the wannabe psycho and Rees the dark horse."

"And Joe the sad, fat closet homosexual," Matt commented.

"Are we all agreed though? You will not plead guilty," Joe told Daniel.

"Yeah."

Daniel met Woods and Brooks the next day.

"So you plan to start your Train to Gain, and shift benefit?" Woods asked.

"I was told I could get extra help in finding employment," Daniel said.

"Good move. I'll speak to Dr McLeish for you. Get him to refer you to your GP. This will all look good, even if you're found guilty," Brooks smiled.

"Which we will try not to have happen," Woods said quickly.

"I almost caved in yesterday," Daniel admitted.

"That's quite normal," Brooks assured him.

"Yeah, even people who are 100 per cent innocent sometimes fear they'll still be found guilty. I've had to talk my share out of changing their plea. Trust me, Daniel if I felt it in your best interest to plead guilty I'd have said so. Having spoken to Jimmy Hatton and Wayne Isaacs I'm pretty sure myself and Mr Brooks here can make Brian Lever out to be the bogeyman. Hague will try to make you out to be wild and unpredictable. I think that will work against him," Woods said.

"How so?" Daniel asked.

"Because, we are trying to make you out to be mentally unstable," Woods replied and Daniel had to smile. "He will of course paint Brian Lever out as a tough but fair type who is liberal to everyone. To be honest that's not the impression I get.

"I'm due to speak to Michelle Fielder in two days and Joe McGinty next week. I have to ask though. Is he a good idea?"

"Why? Because he's unemployed?"

"And a bit of a boozer."

"He's highly intelligent though. He will have a couple of good stories to say about me. I think he might wind Hague up a bit."

"Your decision; also let me assure you of something else," Woods said. "Hague says I'm an office boy. I guess he hasn't checked me out. I'm not boasting here, but I've had a couple of law firms scout me out. I said 'no'."

"Why? That'd be a lot more dosh,"

"Because I enjoy what I do. You think I want to end up an unprincipled bastard like Hague? Besides, how much pressure am I under? They don't expect you to win if you're the defence. But let me assure you myself and Mr Brooks record is all right for winning or persuading the judge to be lenient on the guilty if I think that person deserves it. We're lucky we've got Nolan. She's pretty open minded. But I have to be honest here. She likes to set examples and doesn't believe in going easy on those with hard luck stories."

Lever found himself facing Hague later that day.

"You must understand that he's going for the sympathy vote," Hague said. "I see it quite regularly in criminal law, and I see it all the time in trials against thieving workers."

"What? Making out they had to steal or they felt they deserved it?" Brian asked.

Hague smiled. "Correct, Brian. His not guilty plea is based on pleading temporary insanity. They can prove he had psychological issues I have no doubt of that-"

"Not my problem was it?" Brian interrupted.

"If I may, Mr Lever? What they will be hard pressed to prove is that he was not aware of his actions or the consequences. It's what the plea is based on. For a person to be legally insane they have to be completely unaware of their actions or the consequences.

"Now I firmly believe he did not plan to attack you until seconds before he did. And I think he was only unaware of the consequences for himself. He had no thought of what might happen. Frankly I feel he hoped you would have been hurt more by it."

"So you genuinely think he's guilty?"

"As guilty as sin; how are things at the store going?"

"The replacement manager is one of those types who does a lot but gets nothing done. He's some young bloke who barely knows what he's doing."

"It will most likely be temporary. How are the staff to you?"

"Some are all right. The stupid, useless ones who liked Daniel either glare at me a lot or avoid me. You say if found guilty Daniel will be sent to prison?"

"*When* he is found guilty, think positively. The answer is yes, I hear. Judge Nolan isn't much for sob stories. I think she will make sure of that."

TWENTY-FOUR

Two weeks had gone by. Daniel had got himself signed onto incapacity benefit although it would take a few weeks for the change to be made. He had re-started on the Train to Gain scheme and felt better, although the trial looming was on his mind a lot.

"Hey, yob!" He suddenly heard and felt a can hit his side. He grunted and looked to see Stuart Berry leaning out of a car window as it sped past with a stupid grin on his face. Daniel kept walking along the street. He was suddenly aware they were coming for a second pass.

The driver yelled, "You old man mugger," Berry shouted, "couldn't fight anyone else, could you?"

They then drove on. Daniel gritted his teeth and walked on to The Duke.

In there, he saw his friend Graham, the one who had been there when he had grabbed Sean Mortimer.

"I'm just getting too much grief," Daniel sighed, and then told Graham what happened.

"You should tell the police about it. These guys giving you grief don't care about what you did. They just want an excuse to start trouble and they're so brave they then drive off," Graham said.

Daniel grinned. "Yeah, that's Stuart Berry. I know the south side of Mansford where I go a lot gets a bad rep, but people are more respectful there."

"There's a lot more crime there."

"Yeah, in certain suburbs. I walk the central area quite happily at night without grief."

"To a lot of people you belong inside," Laurie Handle, a regular in his late fifties suddenly said, smiling his sleazy smile.

"Yeah, and a lot of these people disliked me any way. Like you."

"Well, when I first met you were unemployed. Like now. I tend to think of any unemployed as sponging bastards."

"Yeah, well coming from a man who laid off a lot of workers when his company was doing badly, but still paid himself a whopping great bonus, that's a bit unfair."

"That's business. I don't have to justify myself to you."

"Laurie, leave it, eh?" Graham said.

Laurie nodded and walked past, deliberately kicking Daniel's chair leg as he did.

"Let it go," Graham whispered. He watched Laurie go out the back. "You remember Kevin Rowan don't you?"

"Yeah. Short, big built red headed builder bloke. Just stopped coming here all of a sudden."

"Yeah, that's because of Laurie. Laurie took a dislike to Kevin as he has to you. Laurie barged past him once and Kevin told Laurie that if he'd have been a younger man he would have punched his lights out. Laurie told Jim the landlord Kevin had threatened him. Kevin got banned for it. So watch it with him."

"He's a fucking snitch. The bully boy who picked a fight then lost and went whinging to teacher about the bad boy beating him up."

"Look, you're lucky they never did you for attacking that bloke in here a while back."

"He asked for it."

"Doesn't matter; you're a marked man. If I were you I'd lay low for the next few weeks until the trial."

"Then I'll get bored and depressed,"

"Focus on your gym and karate training. Focus on that course you're now doing. I hate to say it, but, if you do go inside, the karate will be valuable." Daniel looked at him and said nothing.

The next day Daniel went to the police station. He went to the desk.

"Yes, can I help you?" The young PC asked.

"My name's Daniel Steele. Can I speak to DS Rivers?"

"May I ask who you are and why?"

"Yes, my name is Daniel Steele. DS Rivers said to see him about any issues. He is my investigating officer."

"I'll see what I can do, Mr Steele."

Daniel sat on a chair and waited. After a few minutes a tall blonde-haired man in a suit and with a contemptuous look on his face walked out.

"I'm DS Warren Hampson," he said, appearing bored. "What do you want?"

"I was hoping to speak to DS Rivers."

"He's been told not to talk to you."

"I see. Can I talk to you then?"

"I'm here aren't I?" Hampson pointed at a side room. "In there."

Hampson followed Steele into the room and closed the door.

"Great. I've got a trial coming up. I've got people giving me a lot of grief about it. I don't want them arrested, just talked to."

"Are they harassing you about what you did?"

"Yeah."

"Good, you deserve it."

Daniel felt angry. "Look, I'm trying to sort my act out, that sort of comment doesn't help."

"And what would you have me do?"

"Get them talked to. Please. They're making my life harder."

"You expect us to help someone who attacked an old man for doing his job."

"Can't you – I mean won't you do anything?"

"Only thing I'd say we can do is put you in custody until the trial."

"You mean prison?"

"Yes, that's right. You belong there any way."

"So you'd arrest a boxer for defending himself against an attacker, but you won't stop people from harassing someone."

"Some would. I won't. I'm the one now who deals with you if you have any other enquiries."

"So you won't help then?"

"Why should I? Your lot harassed the victim."

"He's no victim!" Daniel snapped. "He's a manipulative nasty bully."

"If you say so."

"I'm wasting my time talking to a fucking ignorant prick like you."

Hampson whistled. "Daniel, outbursts like that will not look good at your trial now will they?"

Daniel glared hard at him. "If you say so," he said, and walked out.

Outside he dug out his phone and called Ricky.

"Hello, mate, when's your house bash?... Really, weekend before my trial... Well, it could be one of my last bashes for a while, I'll have to make the most of it... All right, cheers, see ya." He hung up.

Daniel took Graham's advice and did a lot of gym and karate training. If ever he needed an incentive the thought of prison worked. He remembered hearing that Rees had had to learn to be tough in prison. He still went out twice a week on average and focused a lot on his Train to Gain course that he had started.

When Rivers returned to work he was told to watch himself; that he was off Daniel's case until the trial when he would present evidence and Burroughs warned him she would be in court.

The Saturday before the trial, Ricky had Daniel, Matt and Joe around his house.

"So you've been working more on this video tape?" Matt grinned.

"What's it all about?" Joe asked.

Ricky smiled. "You'll see. Me and Daniel have put some work into it."

"Yeah. You remember last August, when we were last round Ricky filmed it? We edited it," Daniel put in.

They sat cracking open beers as Ricky sorted it out to show the film. He sat back.

"OK then, here we go boys," he smirked.

Ricky came up on screen in a suit.

"Hello," the Ricky on screen said. "Welcome to the Ricky Report. As you know, we expose people for what they really are. Today we expose the feared Neo-Nazi leader – Joe McGinty."

"What!" Joe shouted. Matt shushed him.

On screen Ricky continued. "Joe McGinty is a feared racist and homophobe who has made his feelings well known. However tonight we expose him as actually being – a rampant homosexual himself who indulges in sexual intercourse with male prostitutes."

"Wh-at!" Joe shouted. "Yeah, you're a funny cunt Ricky. And you're a dead cunt too!"

"Here we present a witness who is in shadow and has had his voice altered for fear of reprisal," Ricky said on-screen.

The picture changed to show a person in shadow.

"Is that you Daniel?" Matt asked.

Daniel nodded.

The video continued. "Have you been paid to perform sexual acts with Joe McGinty?" on-screen Ricky asked.

"Yes," acting Daniel said in a faked nervous voice.

"And he frequently paid for this service did he?"

"He did. One time he paid two hundred pounds to have ten males, one after the other."

Matt burst out laughing.

"Shut up, nig-nog," Joe said, looking embarrassed. Matt slapped him around the head.

The video continued.

"Was he the giver or receiver?"

"He liked to take it in turns. Sometimes he paid for a threesome so he could have both."

"Oh you cunts," Joe muttered.

"Is it true he used to like to say, quote 'Bend me over and call me Colin'?"

"Yes, frequently." Then it cut back to Ricky. "Joe McGinty was shortly arrested for this. I interviewed him. Clearly he felt he now had nothing to lose.

"I asked him, will you frequently be having intercourse in the prison showers?"

The video cut to Joe. "Of course, what kind of a stupid question is that?"

Daniel sighed.

"Sorry, I made this before…" Ricky said, pausing the video.

"It's all right mate. I'm not going to prison anyway," Daniel forced a smile.

"Keep watching. The next bits are offensive," Ricky smiled.

"I can't imagine who to," Joe sighed. "Ricky, you're dead if this video gets out. Half that lot down The Seal are so thick, they'd probably think it was real."

"Oh, I'm going to put it on YouTube," Matt grinned.

"Don't even think about it," Joe shot back.

Ricky pressed 'play'.

"Mr McGinty, when you were arrested, what were you doing?" Ricky asked on-screen. It cut to Joe. "Tossing myself off."

"I see. Over what?"

It cut back to Joe, "over all those queers out there." Laughs burst out.

Back to Ricky: "Mr McGinty, when freed from prison will you get a male sexual partner?"

"As many as I can get,"

Ricky continued with this line of questioning in the video. "Who would your ideal partner be? Someone you really empathise with. Someone just like you?"

"Some total fucking paedo fag."

Ricky quickly paused it as Daniel and Matt burst out laughing. Joe smiled embarrassed.

"Did you know about this part?" Joe asked Daniel.

Daniel shook his head and tried to stop laughing. "Only the bit I did."

"I think it's time for a cigarette after all that." Matt tried to stop laughing.

"I'll come too, get away from these two wankers," Joe said.

"I see." Matt smiled. "Well come on paedo fag, come on paedo fag."

Joe had to smile. "That's Mr Paedo Fag to you, you ill-educated Negro. Now go back to the servant's quarters where you belong."

When they came back in Joe said, "You are the real queer Ricky."

"Why? Are you offering?" Ricky smiled back.

"What? No fuck right off."

"I might just drag you into my backroom."

Joe shook his head. "We go in there, Ricky, one of us is coming out battered and bloody."

"Yeah, that'll be your arse when I've finished," Ricky cracked.

That it did for Matt who was still sniggering about the paedo fag joke. He collapsed to the floor laughing. Daniel went back into his chair laughing.

"Like a pair of kids you lot," Joe sighed. "Watch it with Matt. He might full on shit himself and become see through."

Matt got up and threw a playful punch which Joe dodged. Joe continued. "And then we have Daniel who got beaten up by a girl in karate once."

"What!" Matt exclaimed. "You got beaten up by a girl?"

"No, I injured my foot sparring," Daniel sighed.

"So the girl beat you up?" Joe said.

Matt was laughing hard. "You got beaten up by a girl."

"And now I'm being slated by Matt who gave up karate, because he kept getting hit." Daniel shook his head

"But you got beaten up by a girl." Matt laughed.

"Not very imaginative, are you?" Ricky commented.

"He's black, of course he's not," Joe smirked.

"Seriously, Joe, I'm getting sick of these racist jokes all the time. Besides I've got ten A and B GCSE's, three A-levels and a degree." Matt retorted.

"Let's get back to the tape," Ricky said.

"Do we really have to?" Joe asked.

"Yes." Daniel and Matt said.

Daniel looked over at Matt.

"Oh, I see the old Ned Kelly's grown back, Matt," he said. Joe burst out laughing. Matt looked annoyed.

"What does that mean?" Ricky asked, looking puzzled.

"Belly," Joe explained.

"I worked hard to get rid of it, but being around you lot is so depressing I find myself drinking again," Matt retorted.

Hours later when they had all gone to sleep. Ricky in his bed, Matt on the sofa and Joe was so drunk he'd passed out on the floor, Daniel sat on his own in the kitchen, a can of beer in front of him.

"This could be my last weekend of freedom," he mumbled to himself.

TWENTY-FIVE

It was Tuesday, the day before the trial was set to begin. Daniel sat in Woods' office. Woods put a cup of tea in front of him.

"Thanks," Daniel breathed.

"It starts tomorrow," Woods said. "Four day trial all being well."

"And then how long do the jury get?"

"As long as it takes. I doubt it will be a verdict they're all agreed on, but a majority verdict. We don't want a quick verdict."

"I do."

"No, you don't Daniel. A quick verdict is likely to be a guilty one." He clasped his hands. "I have to be honest, Daniel, I've removed Michelle Fielder."

"What? Why?"

"Hague will tear her apart over the rape trial. He will ruin her credibility and maybe her to. We still have four character witnesses which is enough and Dr McLeish."

"It's weird Hague hasn't tried to bring in his own psychiatrist to assess me."

"Hague's an over confident, arrogant idiot. He's convinced he can win easily. His problem is he's used to open and shut cases."

"Can we win?"

"I can't and won't promise it as I've said before. But we have a good chance, Daniel. When you walk into that court room tomorrow at half one, you must believe it."

"You know that Brian considers himself hard, but fair?"

"Yes, I think in his own mind he is. If he was still running a company, I'd say he was. But he's not now is he?"

Despite his parents urging him to stay in, Daniel had to go out. The tension of the impending trial was too much for him.

Joe, Ricky, Evan and Pete had come down from The Seal to a place called The Oak Tree. Later they would go to The Duke.

"Let's keep the trial talk down. We're here for a good time," Pete said. "Just remember what I told you, Dan. Also, if you get strung out, just think of Evan's funny shaped nose." Evan looked embarrassed. "What's wrong with my nose? It's all right!"

"Compared to someone who's had an amputation!" Joe cracked. "And then there's Ricky's homosexuality ."

"You'd certainly like that, wouldn't you?" Ricky grinned, sliding an arm around Joe.

"I certainly wouldn't, gay boy," Joe replied.

"I've had enough of all this gay shit," Ricky said, and suddenly grabbed Joe in a body lock and pretended to force himself on him.

"What the -" Joe gasped. "Get off me. Get off me. Oh, why are you so strong?"

"Maybe if you put your pint down you'd be able to get him off," Daniel commented.

Ricky let the stunned looking Joe go.

Joe looked around at them all. "Did you all see that?" he demanded. "Ricky, you really are fucked in the head."

Joe put his left hand on the table. "Pete'd enjoy that. Not me though." Pete thumped Joe's hand. Joe went back clutching it.

"I'll miss all this if I go inside," Daniel sighed.

"You stupid bastard, that's not going to happen," Evan grinned.

"Here, neck some relaxation." Joe tapped Daniel's pint glass, and Daniel complied. Joe then went up to buy drinks.

Later, they walked the ten minutes to The Duke. The night was going well for Daniel, until after an hour he went into the toilet. As he was washing his hands he was aware of two people standing behind him.

"Kyle, Stuart. Where did you two come from?" Daniel breathed.

"I saw you come in," Kyle commented. "But decided to leave you alone. We're out the back with Michelle and that."

"Yeah, I've been telling them all about the plastic chorizo incident," Stuart sneered. "They all think it's pretty funny. I don't think this lot like you much." Kyle smirked. "They're going to bang you up where you belong, aren't they? An oldie basher like you deserves it. Then when you come out, we'll all remember. Your life here is wrecked."

"Not that it wasn't before." Stuart smirked. "You're just a failure. Face it." He then pushed Daniel back.

"What's the matter? Is it because you know I'll fight back?"

"I'm not stupid enough to do that." Daniel tried to walk past, but Kyle threw him back.

"We're still talking to you," Kyle said condescendingly.

"You're just too much of a coward to fight back, aren't you?" Stuart leered, stepping closer.

"I can't."

"But I can," a voice suddenly said. Evan stood in the doorway. A fierce look on his face. He looked hard at Stuart. "You stand there, not so brave now are you?"

"What's it to you?" Kyle demanded. "He's a criminal."

"No, he's a mate. Let him go."

They allowed Daniel to slide past. Evan patted his shoulder reassuringly as he did.

"You two are pussies, you know that?" Evan said. He followed Daniel back to the table.

"Pair of faggots," Evan snarled.

"What happened?" Joe asked.

"I just caught two people threatening Daniel in the toilets," Evan replied.

"Who?" Joe demanded.

"Don't even think about it," Daniel said desperately. "The last thing I need is cozzas here the night before."

"Yeah, he's right," Pete said. "It's best to let it go. We'd better move on before it kicks off again though."

Suddenly, Michelle stormed up to the table. "Is that right?" she demanded.

"Is what right?" Daniel asked.

"You and one of your friends just threatened Kyle and Stuart?"

"They were hassling me!" Daniel gasped.

"I had to step in," Evan added.

"I don't believe either of them would do that. You disgust me, Daniel. I wouldn't testify for you now, even if I could." She stormed off.

"Now that I will not let slide!" Daniel got up and walked quickly out the back.

"Shit, you three stay here," Pete ordered his friends. He followed Daniel.

Daniel found Stuart and Kyle with Michelle and some others.

"Do yourself a favour and clear off," Kyle snapped.

"I was about to, until I found out you poisoned Michelle against me!" Daniel exploded. "Were you just jealous that another bloke could be her friend too, eh?"

"I don't want anything to do with you, you're not what I thought you were," Michelle said nervously, hugging up to Kyle.

"I think she's made her feelings clear," Kyle said.

"Oh, you fucker." Daniel moved closer, and was suddenly aware of Pete grabbing hold of him.

"Leave it, leave it. If you so much as push one of them it goes against you," Pete whispered.

Stuart got up, sensing it was safe. "Yeah, get out of here." Evan suddenly charged around the corner. He grabbed the stunned Stuart, and right hooked him in the ribs, before pinning him down.

"You feeling tough now, you cunt?" Evan growled.

"Get inside," Pete told Daniel.

"Yeah, Kyle's your fucking HERO, isn't he?" Daniel yelled at Michelle before going in.

Pete grabbed Evan and pulled him off. Evan gave surprisingly low resistance.

"You put your phone away!" Pete ordered a middle aged man. "Don't even think about calling the police."

The man nodded and did as he was told. Stuart was gasping, clutching his ribs. Michelle looked terrified, as did Kyle and most of the others outside.

Pete glared at Stuart. "Just remember if you snitch, Daniel will do you for harassment."

Stuart nodded desperately.

"Rest assured, we're leaving now," Pete said. "This man here won't need an ambulance. And don't any of you even think about calling the police, because they won't care about a pub fight, trust me here. I know."

"Can we just get away from these arrogant fuckers?" Evan demanded.

"Yeah, I'd say that was a good idea. Let's go."

TWENTY-SIX

Daniel's alarm clock went off at ten the next morning. Sitting up in bed, he turned it off and sat there. It felt so weird. Like it wasn't real. Today was the day it all started. In a week's' time he could be waking up in a prison cell. No, he forced that thought from his mind.

His parents were already up and about. They gave him nervous greetings and smiles. His mother made him some breakfast. He ate, and then shaved the stubble he had allowed to grow so he was clean shaven. Then he showered. As he finished putting on his suit his phone rang. It was Joe.

"All right Joe," he answered.

"How you holding up, buddy?" Joe asked.

"Trying to force the idea of prison out of my head."

"Yeah, I'm trying to force Ricky's video tape out of mine, piss taking prick. Matt obviously has nothing better to do, the last two days he keeps sending me stupid texts, like 'Is that Paedo or Mr Fag?' and 'Do you wear Paedo's to swim in?'"

Daniel laughed. "You've got it harder."

"Seriously though, we're all behind you. Everyone not out last night sends their best, even Alan. We want you to know we'll be there if possible for the verdict."

"Thanks, I appreciate that. I got to go now. Is it Thursday you give evidence?"

"Yeah, about what a terrible bloke you are. No, seriously though mate, just sit and look pretty until you have to speak."

"See ya," Daniel clicked off.

Little was said during the drive to the court. They walked through the entrance. To his relief, Daniel didn't see Brian upon arrival. Security checked them and then Daniel was taken to a private room where he sat with three guards, two male, and one female, and waited. Finally the tannoy announcement came.

"All for the trial of Mr D O Steele to court two."

Daniel breathed deeply. So much had happened since that fateful day. Now it was time.

He stood and walked slightly ahead of the guards. One of the male guards walked forward and opened the door leading to the dock. Daniel walked through and sat on the hard backed chair in front of him. The guards took up positions behind him. They seemed relaxed. They doubted he'd be trouble.

To Daniel's right was the public gallery, where he had no doubt Brian Lever's family and friends would be. Daniel doubted Brian had any friends out of work. Ahead, to his right, Hague sat looking at his notes. Daniel knew that his family were to his left. His brother and sister had come for this, both taking time off work on compassionate grounds. In front of them were Woods and Brooks. Woods turned around and walked up to him.

"You OK?" he whispered.

"I'm trying not to think too much," Daniel grinned nervously.

"Smart move. Brian Lever is the first one in. If he glares at you, don't look back."

"Who else?"

"Paul Hirst and Aisha Abbas. I won't be asking Hirst anything, there's no point, but did you say Aisha liked you?"

"Yeah."

"Right then. Plus, Hague is going to show the security camera footage of the incident." Woods smiled and walked back to his seat.

The clerk, a tall thin middle aged man spoke loudly. "All rise."

Judge Abigail Nolan strode to her seat. "Please sit ladies and gentlemen," she said. "Please stand Mr Steele,"

Daniel had remained standing anyway, as advised by Woods and Pete.

The clerk said, "Are you Daniel Oliver Steele?"

"Yes sir."

"Thank you. Mr Steele, you may sit," The clerk replied.

Daniel sat.

The members of the jury were then sworn in. Daniel looked at them, trying to imagine who might be sympathetic, and who wouldn't. Seven of the twelve were men, three young and four middle aged. Two of the young men were smartly dressed but casual, the other wore a suit. Three of the middle aged men wore suits, while the other just wore a T-shirt and jeans. Of the five women two were young and both smartly dressed, the three older women were also smartly dressed. None of their faces betrayed anything

"Mr Hague, you may proceed," Judge Nolan said.

Hague stood grandly and gave the jurors a smile. Here we go, Daniel thought.

"Ladies and gentlemen of the jury, my name is George Hague and I am representing the Crown versus Daniel Steele. The defendant is accused on the eleventh of January this year of launching a brutal and pre-meditated assault on Brian Francis Lever in the Fast Service store that Steele was once employed by. Despite having turned himself in and fully admitting to the offence Daniel Steele has pleaded not guilty to the assault on the grounds of ill mental health."

"Alleged assault," Nolan corrected sharply. "Mr Steele has not yet been found guilty."

"Much obliged, your honour." Hague nodded. "Apologies members of the jury. My duty however is to prove beyond reasonable doubt that the defendant was fully aware of what was going on at the time; that he was angry at the treatment he had received at the Fast Service store he worked in, and looked to take it out on a man more than thirty years his senior. All this, I will explain in time, but to make it brief, the prosecution will prove that the defendant was very unhappy with his hours and while some of you may sympathise or even empathise, just remember that the hours we sometimes all have to work are a misfortune of life, and also it does not justify deciding to take it out on someone, as indeed the prosecution will prove that Mr Steele did. I wish to call my first witness, the victim of the alleged assault, Mr Brian Lever."

Brian walked into the witness stand, in a smart suit. He leant forward slightly and fixed Daniel with the familiar glare he had constantly given him when they had worked together. Daniel turned away. The clerk swore Brian in.

"Mr Lever, before we get to the incident that took place, I would like to go over your background."

"Of course," Brian said.

"Good. You have worked for five years at the Mansford Fast Service store since taking early retirement, am I correct?"

"Yes."

"You were previously a director with Joseph-Bowen engineering firm. Is that correct?

"It is."

"And you retired of your own free will. You were not dismissed or forced out. Is that true?"

"It is."

"And you have no criminal convictions, have you?"

"None,"

"So members of the jury, this man is of good character," Hague told the jury and then turned back to Brian. "Mr Lever, could you describe the relationship between yourself and Daniel Steele?"

"I consider myself an experienced and good judge of character. I disliked him the day he started. He had got the job on the pretence of having done it before, when he had not.

He was slow to learn, no very slow, not to mention lazy and he complained a lot."

"Really? How so?"

"After a few weeks he was griping to me about having to do every weekend early starts. I told him, if he didn't like it to quit. He persisted and I just kept giving him that answer."

"That's understandable. You once caught him doing Nazi salutes behind your back did you not?"

"Yes, I was disgusted. I reported him to Mark Edmunds the manager, who did no more than tell him off. All the then manager cared about was filling the hours."

"He was also known for verbal rants, wasn't he?"

Yes, I'd hear it as well, as did my colleagues," He looked at Nolan.

She smiled politely.

"And now to the incident itself, I take it you are able to talk about it?"

"I certainly am!" Brian snapped.

"That's good to hear. Now please state your version of events of what occurred on the eleventh of January."

"I had opened the shop and taken in the morning delivery with colleagues, one of which was Daniel Steele." Brian said. "Somewhere along the line I became aware that Steele had made a mistake. I discovered some new stock of eggs had been put out as opposed to the older ones out the back and Miss Abbas the other supervisor told me it was Daniel who put them out. I called him over and demanded to know why he had put new stock out when there was older out back."

"Yes, I understand you claimed he should have been aware. Do you feel it may have been wrong to directly blame him?"

Daniel's eyes widened with surprise, so did Brian's.

"What?" Brian asked, stunned.

"That maybe your frustrations against him boiled over in that moment in time?"

That makes more sense, Daniel thought.

Brian grimaced. "It could well be. I'd put up with a lot from him."

"So what happened next?"

"He started arguing – as usual. I told him what he was to do. He then lost it and punched me in the face and the belly, and threw me against the milk fridge."

"And then?"

"I'm not sure. I came to in the staff room."

"So he obviously hit you hard enough to not knock you out, but enough to lose your awareness. If you can remember, did he seem highly agitated to you in the time immediately before the alleged assault?"

"To answer the question: no more than usual. He was still drunk from the night before too. He was always out drinking until the early hours and then turning up a few hours later."

"I see, so from your observation the likelihood is he was drunk and aggressive," Hague smiled.

"Objection. Your honour, that's presumption only," Brooks said, standing.

"It's me putting the witness's last statement into words," Hague said quickly.

"I'm going to sustain it," Nolan said. "But I will allow that Mr Steele may have been under the influence. Any further questions Mr Hague?"

"Yes, Mr Lever, when you say 'drunk'. How would you say that was so? Did his breath smell? Was he walking erratically?"

"I didn't notice either. But then again I wasn't looking for that. I had heard him joking with someone when he first arrived that he had been out until a few hours ago and still felt a little on the wasted side'. That was roughly what he said."

"Your honour if I may." Brooks stood. "There are no other witnesses to that, its hearsay surely?"

"Mr Lever is a most credible witness, plus the defendant openly admitted to being out the night before," Hague replied.

Nolan weighed it up. "I'll allow it. Any further questions Mr Hague?"

"No, your honour. Thank you, Mr Lever." Hague sat.

Brooks stood. Daniel forced himself to stay calm. He saw Brian staring hard at his defence.

"Mr Lever, are you sure you're of good previous character?" Brooks said bluntly.

"Of course I am."

"Are you? If that is so then why have so many complaints been made against you in the Fast Service store in the last five years? Going over your record I count eleven complaints."

"Look, I'm hard, but fair."

"Well, yes, you most certainly are. Hard on those you dislike and fair to those you do."

"I only have a problem with those who are not up to the standards I set."

"Like Daniel Steele? Whom you were against from day one as you felt he lied on his application form."

"He had. He claimed he'd done the same kind of job before."

"To you personally?"

"No, to Mark Edmunds, the store manager, who told me."

"If you'd have bothered to check, Mr Lever you would have seen that Mr Steele had worked in a supermarket on Food Service counters, so out of pure assumption you victimised him."

"Your honour, I must object to this," Hague snapped.

"No, over ruled," Nolan replied. She turned her head and ignored Hague throw his arms up in disgust.

"No, no answer, Mr Lever," Brooks chided. "Just like your assumption he was drunk on the morning he allegedly assaulted you. Was he stumbling around, or slurring his speech?"

"As I said no, but I remember he never denied it when I confronted him about it just before he attacked me."

"Your honour, I object again, let's get to the point," Hague said angrily.

"Sustained. Please get to your point Mr Brooks."

"Very well. Let's talk about the Nazi salute incident. A very rude and disrespectful bit of behaviour by the defendant. Why had he done it?"

"I told him off about something."

"And do you remember him trying to explain about his learning disability?"

"Yes, and I told him that was all a load of rubbish and not to waste my time with it."

"So could that be why he got so angry?"

"How about the amount of times he made me angry at him!"

"Yes," Brooks looked at his sheet of paper. "Like the time you threw a box at him, the times you rammed the cage of goods he was pulling, which I might add is the way he had been taught to do so in the supermarket. The times you stamped through him like he wasn't there. The way you snapped his name out and expected him to come running. To me, it sounds like a severe case of bullying in the workplace."

"Your honour, that is no justification for assault," Hague said.

"Mr Brooks?" Nolan asked.

"The points will all add up," Brooks explained calmly. "Now Mr Lever, do you deny any of these incidents and please remember; you're under oath. Do you deny any of them?"

"No," Brian said quietly. "But I don't have to justify myself. Daniel Steele was a waste of space, maybe if he'd have come to work and not been out drinking he might have performed better."

"Oh, do you think it wrong for a twenty-four-year old to go out with his friends on a Friday and Saturday night?" Brooks smiled.

"Don't answer, that's irrelevant," Nolan said sternly.

"I'll withdraw the question," Brooks said. "So you don't believe in learning difficulties?"

"I don't think they're an excuse."

"Even though people trained in the field do? And although it is widely accepted that mental health problems affect concentration."

"That's up to them."

"So you're against people who have problems, no, a disability in fact?"

"I am not!"

"But you made the defendant feel very bad because of his problems?"

"It's not a charity, it's a business,"

"Really? So people with special needs shouldn't be there, even if they were committed and hard working?"

"It's not my problem."

"So what would be fair? Should they be pushed out the way and put on benefits all their lives?"

"No, I'm against anyone who's unemployed."

"Well what should be done with them? What should happen to them?"

"I refuse to answer," Brian snarled.

"Mr Brooks," Nolan said. "Your point is made. Let's move on."

"Much obliged, your honour," Brooks smiled, and then turned back to Brian. "So, do you consider intimidating behaviour, like walking around with an angry look on your face appropriate for a harmonious work place?"

"It keeps them alert, it keeps them on their toes," Brian protested. It was clear he was getting agitated.

"For people that are paid just over minimum wage, even when, I might add, they are doing hours that might hinder them having a reasonable life!" Brooks suddenly snapped.

"That's tough. If they don't like it, they can quit."

"Perhaps I'm going about this the wrong way," Brooks gave him an almost friendly smile. "It may surprise you to hear this, but I don't think you deserved to be attacked."

"You could have fooled me."

"My apologies if that is so. You see, Mr Steele was a man on the edge, having been through his various traumas, and hardships of being a slow learner. I feel that maybe you had the misfortune of pushing him too far – through no fault of your own except for your way of thinking."

"He knew what he was doing."

"You were a director of a firm which had highly motivated and trained workers, yes?"

"That's right.

"So, certainly coming to a place where a lot of employees are badly trained and low in motivation would be a shock to you would it not?"

"Yes."

"So, Mr Lever, your attitude was one reflective on your previous occupation. Perhaps inappropriate for those who lack motivation. Your frustrations certainly got the better of you?"

"Constantly. These people who had been hired just to quickly fill a vacancy."

"Like Daniel Steele. Someone who you felt was not up to the job?"

"Definitely."

"So you gave him a hard time whenever you worked with him?"

"Too right."

Brooks smiled. "And finally you just pushed him that little bit too far."

Brian's jaw dropped. He had walked right into the trap.

"Thank you. I have no further questions," Brooks smiled.

"Thank you. You may go, Mr Lever," Nolan said.

Brian gave Daniel one last glare and walked out. Brooks sat back down and Daniel saw him talking to Woods. Daniel thought Brooks had performed well. Making Brian out to be a bully without Brian having even realised he was doing it. Brooks had got the points across without dwelling on them.

Paul Hirst was the next in. He stated what he had seen. Woods and Brooks had obviously had a quick change of heart and Brooks questioned him on how Brian Lever had perhaps gone out of his way to provoke Daniel. Hirst was unsure how to answer and that was all Brooks had wanted.

Aisha Abbas came in after and stated how she had worked with Brian Lever for three years and how he was very efficient and she was then asked by Hague to tell the jury about the assault in detail and how badly hurt Brian was. Nolan finally asked Hague to move it along when Hague made it clear he wanted to dwell on every little detail. Hague ended by talking her through how Daniel had smelt of alcohol from the night before and had seemed still to be mildly drunk. This young supervisor was however, the defence's secret weapon.

"Miss Abbas," Brooks asked. "Am I correct to say that Daniel Steele confided his state of mind to you?"

Aisha looked uncomfortable. "He did."

"Let's expand –"

"Your honour, I must protest. What relevance does this have?" Hague demanded.

"No, I want to see where it is going," Nolan replied.

"Thank you your honour," Brooks said. "Miss Abbas, as Mr Lever said, Daniel was coming in smelling of alcohol in the mornings."

"His evening shifts also," she said.

"So he drank heavily?"

"Not so much that. But he used to state how he felt to me and not just about his shifts."

"He talked about what he had been through?"

"The knife attack? Yes."

"And he told you about wanting to be in therapy?"

"Yes, but Mark Edmunds had denied it"

"And did you feel Brian Lever was always trying to provoke him?"

She fidgeted uncomfortably. "It didn't justify what he did,"

"No. But did Brian Lever behave in a provocative way to him?"

"Yes he did,"

"How so?"

"Just saying things about people being bad at what they did and then glaring at Daniel. Talking about the manager not knowing what he was doing, how he hired wrong people and he would glare at Daniel."

"Your honour, that's enough!" Hague snapped.

"Mr Brooks?" Nolan asked.

"One more question." Brooks said.

"Proceed." Nolan said.

"Do you personally feel the conditions Steele worked in contributed to his state of mind?"

Aisha breathed. "Yes," She said quietly. Hague looked horrified.

"What do you mean?" Brooks asked quickly, before Hague could object.

"The shifts depriving him of therapy, of karate which gave him self-belief and not being able to see much of his friends," she sighed.

"Thank you, Miss Abbas." Brooks smiled.

TWENTY-SEVEN

Walker came up to Sandra Cole's desk.

"Sandra, got a minute?" he asked.

"Sure, what's up?" she asked.

"I think you should talk to Rivers. He'd listen to you."

"About what?"

"He gives evidence tomorrow. We're worried about which way his loyalties will go."

"Didn't Burroughs want you to give evidence?"

"Yeah, but the Super's got faith in Rivers. If Rivers fucks up, that will be him done, Rivers I mean. I'd hate that to happen."

At that moment though, Burroughs came out and asked Rivers, who was on the other side of the office, into her office.

In the office, she sat down, glaring at him.

"Now Sergeant Rivers, against my judgement, you are speaking in court tomorrow. I just think that you should be aware that DC Walker and I will be watching. I might add that DC Walker is concerned about you."

"I appreciate that."

"I don't want you talking liberal rights for special needs people in there." Burroughs continued.

"Ma'am, that's offensive!" Rivers said edgily.

"I find people like Daniel Steele offensive. When my son Ben is working on a university degree in Business Management, my – dyslexic – son."

"Good for your wonderful son! Not all special needs people are the same you know. Plus Steele has trauma issues," Rivers snarled.

"I find excuses being made for personal problems appalling."

"As do I. So I wonder what Brian Lever's excuse for being an arse was."

"He's an honest, hardworking man who was attacked by a disgruntled employee, is that understood?"

"Yes ma'am. That's true, Steele was fed up of his treatment, look ma'am, I will speak against him, but I have no sympathy for men like Lever. Treating special needs people like he did. Steele wasn't the only one you know."

Burroughs rose angrily. "Ben seems to get by just fine!"

"But special needs affects people in different ways. Some get by, some don't. There are so many different factors."

"Enough, OUT, NOW," she thundered.

Rivers nodded and walked out.

Daniel wasn't due in court until three that day. He decided to take a walk at about twelve to Major's Hardware to visit his friend Andy. Hague had shown the jury the security tape of the assault the previous afternoon. He had made a big deal about how the first punch was a clear martial arts punch. How only a person well trained in unarmed combat could have delivered that. Daniel had felt a bit upset watching himself do something like that.

Getting to the store he remembered from when he worked there that Roger was on his lunch break in the neighbouring pub at that time. He was hoping that Miles Booth was at lunch to. Walking in he saw Andy instantly. Sadly Miles was there also.

"All right, Andy?"

"All right, what brings you here?"

"Just thought I'd say hello. How are things?"

"Same old, same old."

"Ask how things are with him," Miles put in.

Daniel looked at him, and then faced Andy. "I'm in court later, second day of the trial."

"How'd the first day go?" Andy asked.

"Hard to say. My barrister did pretty well on cross examinations," Daniel grinned. "They're known as the 007's, my solicitor and barrister 'cos their names are Woods and Brooks Double 'OO'."

"So our taxes are about to pay for you to go away are they?" Miles demanded.

"Come on, Miles, don't," Andy said.

But Daniel was now glaring at him. "I remember working here how you were always rude when I couldn't find things. Saying 'what can't you find now, Daniel?'"

"Yes, after eight weeks it defied belief you not being able to find things."

"It wasn't intentional. I can't help it. I used to walk around trying to work out where things went, remember?"

"And you still couldn't," Miles sighed. "So our taxes paid for you to be off work then and now. Then you'll be in prison which will cost us more."

"I didn't ask to have learning difficulties and mental health problems that affect my concentration. Where do you get off on being like this?" Daniel demanded.

"As a man of my principles I must -"

"Principles?" Daniel looked stunned. "You are the most vindictive, ignorant, judgemental, pompous and arrogant person, you know that?"

Miles was lost for words.

"Leave the man alone," a middle aged male customer said to Daniel.

Daniel glared at Miles. "Miles Booth: the most racist, prejudiced person I know. He's no man." Daniel patted Andy on the shoulder and walked out.

Nearly three hours, later Daniel sat in the dock, with the three guards behind him. He could hear bits of chatter from his right and recognised Brian's voice occasionally. Woods and Brooks entered slightly before Hague, who smiled in the direction of the public gallery, before turning to his notes. Woods approached Daniel.

"Mark Edmunds is in first, he received a court subpoena, ordering him in," Woods whispered. "As you can imagine he never wanted to come."

"Is he being charged with what he did?" Daniel whispered back.

Woods nodded. "Witness intimidation and attempting to pervert the course of justice. Fast Service has cut him off. They don't want anything to do with him. He's looking at a bit of time in prison, and he will find it hard to ever get a decent job again. Given how he abused his position of trust."

"I'm not vindictive – but, that's fine by me. Who else?"

"DS Rivers; now I remember what you said about him, and don't worry, it won't be brought up, your chat with him in The Duke, but Brooks will ask him as a 'fellow dyspraxic' how he feels about your treatment," Woods returned to his seat.

"All rise," the clerk stated.

The formalities were gone through. Then Nolan turned to Hague who looked uncomfortable. "Please call your next witness," she said.

"Very well, your honour. The court calls Mark Edmunds."

Daniel had not seen Edmunds since the day before the attack. Edmunds walked into the witness box and was sworn in. Hague faced him.

"For the benefit of the court I will save Mr Brooks two questions." Hague said. "You are here under subpoena, yes?"

"I am," Edmunds growled.

"And you are currently facing charges of witness intimidation, and attempting to pervert the cause of justice?"

"Yes, that's right," Edmunds glared at Daniel.

"Please refrain from looking at the defendant," Hague told him. "Perhaps you could tell us why you felt it necessary to do this Mr Edmunds?"

"I was running a C-store; it's a very demanding job. Daniel was a malcontent, always unhappy about things, always expecting it to be done for him. He assaulted a man. I didn't feel he deserved any help. I did what I did for the sake of the store I ran. And yes to make my life easier, but who wouldn't? Brian was trouble too, but at least he was efficient."

"Let me clarify then," Hague said. "Lawfully what you did was wrong. But you felt that the defendant, Daniel Steele had no right to a fair trial?"

"Who could? He attacked a 57-year-old man? Would anyone?"

Hague smiled. "Thank you, Mr Edmunds. Did Steele cause a lot of problems for you in the store?"

"Yes, as I said always complaining, and regularly coming in mildly intoxicated. I should have dismissed him much earlier. But him being drunk was the general consensus of the staff present at the time of the attack. I arrived shortly after."

"Thank you. That is all." Hague said.

Daniel was surprised; Hague was appealing to the heart with that. As Hague sat, Brooks rose.

He said, "Mr Edmunds, how would you have assessed Mr Steele's state of mind?"

"I wouldn't, I'm no psychiatrist.

"Your former supervisor Miss Aisha Abbas felt he was mentally unstable."

"I think that she fancied him," Edmunds scoffed.

"Your honour, that's hearsay, surely," Brooks said.

"Yes, agreed. Jurors, please disregard that last statement," Nolan said.

Edmunds looked annoyed. "That's my opinion."

"Unless specified, facts only thank you," Nolan told him.

"And to my next point, you denied him a life with the unsocial hours you kept him on. I have here a timesheet as an example," Brooks continued.

"Tuesday, 3-11pm, Wednesday and Thursday, the same. Friday, off, but no chance to go out at night, Saturday and Sunday, 6am until 2pm. How can a young man have a life with those hours?"

"Job comes first," Edmunds replied.

"Objection your honour. The shifts are irrelevant anyway," Hague cut in.

"Sustained, move on Mr Brooks," Nolan agreed.

"Very well your honour. Is it not true though you denied him psychotherapy when he told you he'd be put on it?"

"He never mentioned it at the interview. And full disclosure is a legal requirement."

"Would you have employed him if he had done so and declared his special needs?"

"No I wouldn't."

"If you know business law, you will realise that is illegal."

"It shouldn't be!" Edmunds snarled.

"Well it is Mr Edmunds," Nolan said sharply.

"Well I told him, he'd have to sort the therapy out in his own time."

"And how, when you kept changing his week day shifts, which I might add were known only up to a fortnight in advance?" Brooks shouted.

"Objection your honour to Mr Brooks' tone of voice," Hague snapped.

"Is my learned friend making a joke?" Brooks demanded. "What we are hearing here is appalling."

"I agree, but lower the tone, Mr Brooks," Nolan smiled.

"My apologies your honour," Brooks said. "Mr Edmunds, how do you justify depriving someone of therapeutic treatment that possibly could have prevented the alleged assault. You're guilty in my opinion of provoking the attack."

"Do you know how hard it is to run a business with all the legislation there is these days?" Edmunds said angrily.

"I appreciate that, but how does that justify obstructing necessary treatment?" Brooks demanded.

"Because he was a stupid fucking idiot, like a lot of my former employees were. Who gives a fuck about some retarded moron like Daniel Steele anyway?" Edmunds exploded.

"One more expletive from you Mr Edmunds and I'll hold you in contempt," Nolan said angrily.

"It's all right, your honour, that's all I have to say." Brooks smiled.

"Witness is excused," Nolan snarled at Edmunds, and then after he had left she said more pleasantly, "I think we need a recess after that, twenty minutes,"

Tony Partt stood just outside the court room with Brian Lever and his wife Cheryl. Hague approached them.

"We were just saying Mr Hague how the defence is doing surprisingly well for a pair of 'office boys' as you rated them," Partt smiled.

"Oh surely you're not worried," Hague retorted. "It's hardly what you'd call rocket science, the defence he is using. I'll beat him, don't you worry."

Cheryl Lever said, "Well this Woods had an offer from the company I work for. They rated him as a very promising solicitor."

"So why's he doing what he's doing?" Hague looked confused.

"He obviously likes what he does," Mrs Lever said.

"You fucking idiot!" Partt growled. "Did you check his credentials? No, you just assumed he was some kid just out of university didn't you?"

Hague looked embarrassed. "Well, I – "

"You might lose this," Brian snarled.

Hague regained his composure. "Look, I will win. I have plenty of ammunition which I will not tell you about here. You might feel that Woods is winning at present, but he won't be for long,"

Woods and Daniel had stayed in the court room and he was telling Daniel how things were working out nicely.

"If we have the jury find you not guilty you will just be ordered to continue your treatment," Woods ended.

TWENTY-EIGHT

Walker and Burroughs watched Rivers enter the court and go to the witness box to be sworn in.

"I don't get the super's logic here, ma'am, with no disrespect meant," Walker whispered.

"Me neither," Burroughs agreed. "But Rivers knows he will be suspended and put on review if he behaves stupidly today."

Rivers breathed deeply as he turned to face Hague who smiled at him.

"Your credentials are excellent, Sergeant," Hague started. "You made DS at thirty-one having only served several years on the police force. Your investigative record is also impeccable."

"Thank you," Rivers nodded.

"Members of the jury, my apologies, this is a very boring but very necessary part of the trial." Hague grinned and waited for the laughs to fade. "But I implore you to please pay attention; this is very relevant to the Crown," He turned back to face Rivers.

"Sergeant Rivers, you are head of the investigation, correct."

"Yes sir, I am."

Hague then took him through the details of the investigation, the alleged assault, and the physical effects on Brian Lever. He then moved on.

"Is it not true that you received a complaint by Mr Lever that he was harassed in the workplace by two of Daniel Steele's friends?"

"Yes, but we were unable to find any connection to Mr Steele and the two involved."

"I'm sorry, what do you mean?"

"Oh, we were unable to prove that he had any involvement."

"I see. Having dealt with the defendant, what were your first impressions of him?"

Rivers felt Burroughs' eyes boring into him. "He was very reluctant to talk. He seemed to feel no remorse for what he had done. He seemed to feel that the victim deserved it."

Daniel stared at the floor. Rivers had not lied. He was the enemy.

"He had felt the victim 'deserved' it." Hague faced the jury. "Hardly the thought of someone in a bad state of mind." He turned back to Rivers. "The defendant also keeps very bad company, yes?"

"Yes, many of his close associates have previous convictions."

"For violence?"

"All of the convicted ones do, yes."

"The defence contends that he was 'pushed over the edge'. I feel it could be more a result of peer pressure into attacking a person who is seen as an enemy."

"Objection," Brooks said. "That's hearsay."

"I'll allow it," Nolan said. "Please continue Sergeant Rivers."

"I'd say it's a possibility, yes. I did have dealings with Mr Steele's associates during the investigation. That struck me as their mentality," Rivers answered.

"And why were you having dealings with them?" Hague asked.

"DC Walker, DC Spears and I wanted to make sure that no witness intimidation would happen. None did."

"As a result of your presence?"

"I can't say, sir. Maybe."

"Was Mr Steele tested for levels of alcohol upon arrest?"

"The arresting officers tested him and found that he had a level of alcohol still. Taking into account that the assault had been roughly an hour previously the level would have been slightly reduced."

"Thank you Sergeant Rivers, I have no further questions." Hague smiled.

In the public gallery Walker whispered, "He's holding up well, isn't he?"

"So far," Burroughs replied, her eyes on Rivers.

Brooks rose. He kept looking at a sheet of paper, before looking at Rivers.

"Sergeant Rivers, as my learned friend has said your police and investigative credentials are superb. I will not be questioning you on the investigation itself. Please confirm your name as Michael Dean Rivers."

"Yes, sir. That is me."

"Are you the same Michael Dean Rivers who eleven years ago was admitted to the Stratton Psychiatric Institute?"

"Your honour, this has no relevance," Hague shot up.

"But it will, I can assure you," Brooks smiled.

Nolan hesitated. "Proceed," she said. Hague threw his arms up in disgust. "Mr Hague! I will not have that in my court room. Do you understand?"

"Yes, Your Honour. My sincerest apologies," Hague said, looking annoyed.

"Please answer Sergeant Rivers," Nolan said gently. "I realise this may be a sensitive issue."

"Yes, that was me, Rivers sighed. "It was very close, me making it into the police years later."

"I find it very interesting that they allowed it. Maybe because of why you were admitted," Brooks said.

"I will try to be as sensitive as I can, Sergeant Rivers. I am sorry if you find this hard. Why were you admitted?"

"I had suffered a nervous break-down."

"And what triggered that?"

"Previous employment."

"Please specify."

Rivers gasped loudly, then said, "I had been subjected to severe harassment and bullying for having special needs. I had been pushed over the edge."

"Like the defendant was you mean?"

"No, I never assaulted anyone."

"You certainly did not, but you were pushed to a breakdown by the treatment. So Sergeant I will ask you, as you are under oath, should Daniel Steele be found guilty?"

Rivers looked dazed. "Yes, he should."

"And do you feel he should go to prison?"

Rivers stared at the floor, and then up to face Brooks. "No, I don't."

Murmurs came from the onlookers.

"And why is that?" Brooks pressed.

"He lost it with the victimisation he received from people, past and present. He'd had enough and he lost it. He was pushed too far and he lost control."

"Your honour, the sergeant is no psychiatrist," Hague said desperately.

"I've seen enough offenders. I know who attacks out of maliciousness, and who is driven to the point they have no conception of what they're doing," Rivers turned and glared in Brian Lever's direction.

"And men like the so-called victim are cruel and sadistic men who just -"

"That's enough, sergeant," Nolan cut in. "You've made your point. As a police officer you are out of order for what you just said."

"You all try being victimised for a disability, automatically blamed for anything going wrong, working hard, but still get made to feel worthless, see what it does to you. It ruined me, and it may ruin Daniel Steele too, while smug types get to walk away with it."

"That's enough, you are excused!" Nolan snapped.

"Tell DS Rivers he's suspended, pending an inquiry," Burroughs said angrily to Walker in the public gallery.

TWENTY-NINE

Rivers stood outside, feeling lost, more lost than he had since his recovery from the break down. He turned and headed for a café that he could see. Suddenly, he felt himself thrown back into a wall, and pushed again into the alleyway by the side of the court. He saw Walker, fury in his eyes. Walker had his hands gripping him just under the collar bone on either side.

"What the fuck was that, Rivers?" Walker demanded angrily.

"That's Sergeant Rivers to you."

"Not anymore. The DI says you're suspended pending an inquiry. That's your whole life thrown away, just because you had to stick up for that idiot in there."

Rivers wrestled Walker's arms off. Despite Walker being four inches taller and broader shouldered, Rivers was far more muscular, and after a few seconds of grappling, Walker let go.

"I remember that Pakistani officer, refused to guard the Israeli embassy, they didn't dismiss him," Rivers pointed out.

"They fucking should have! What's that to do with you, eh?"

"I defended a bloke with special needs who was victimised by -"

Walker turned and suddenly pushed Rivers hard into the wall. "Do you know how much I've been sticking up for you lately? Do you realise what a mug the super will look? He put his faith in you. That's the thanks we get."

Walker turned and clenched his fists, before facing Rivers again. "The storm in that public gallery you've caused. Brian Lever and his family looked like they wanted to lynch me!"

"I said find Steele guilty, didn't I?"

"Yeah, you then said he was the real victim. If he gets off how many criminals will use the excuse they were pushed too far?"

Rivers shrugged. "Fuck it."

"You selfish bastard!" Walker suddenly swung his right fist into Rivers' jaw. It wasn't the hardest punch, but Rivers was surprised and fell back into the wall. "You make me sick – sarge!" Walker turned and stormed away.

Woods came up to Daniel who was in the waiting room.

"Bit of a shocker, eh?" Daniel smiled.

Woods looked grim. "I've just had to talk the judge out of a mistrial."

"Sorry?"

"The judge wanted to dismiss the jury and start again. With DC Walker representing the Crown witness."

"What stopped it?"

"For once I'm grateful to Hague. I said it was unfair on you and Brian Lever to start again. I said you'd both been through a lot of stress in the build-up and it wouldn't be right, that one of you might crack having to go through it again. Hague agreed with me. As I added, it was just Rivers' opinion got out of hand."

"That's a relief. I couldn't face waiting again, you know?" Daniel looked ahead. "I feel bad for DS Rivers, but I'm glad he said what he did."

"It's called self-preservation. It's nothing to be ashamed of, Daniel. I hate to say this but I think Hague had ulterior motives. Rivers still said you should be found guilty even though he went into one on your behalf."

Brooks came in. "They're ready to start."

"Not much we can do with the next two I'm afraid." Woods smiled. "It's the doctor who treated Brian who has X-rays and everything and the first officer on the scene after the assault."

Rivers walked for ages until he arrived at Major's Hardware. He walked in and saw Roger Major and Miles Booth talking.

"Oh, it's you," Miles said tiredly. "Daniel was in here earlier, mouthing off at me. We're going to try a restraining order."

"What did he say?" Rivers asked.

"That I was pompous and arrogant," Miles smiled. "Me? At least I earn my dough. At least I'm good at what I do. And he insulted me!"

Rivers nodded and then said, "Good."

"Now, hold on -" Miles said stunned.

Rivers stepped closer. "Did it piss you off Miles, that he was trying to better himself? Did it annoy you that through study he might have found his calling and achieved things?"

"No, it annoyed me that he wasted my taxes by getting benefits."

Rivers acted like Miles had not spoken. "Maybe he could have used his new qualifications had he got them to get a decent, well paid job, while you are a thirty-five-year-old man who can't survive without his parents, a sad tosser with no friends or social life or career ambitions. It just reminded you of what a sad fucked up loser you are!"

"Now that's enough. Get out!" Roger snapped.

Rivers turned his anger on Roger. "And you dismissed him. Why? Because keeping him on made your life a little harder. Because it made your life inconvenient. Because you're an idle cunt who likes to spend two hours a day in the pub, and when you are here you just like to wander around chatting. Oh, you say he's a lovely lad and you want to help him out. So why not at least give him an extended review period?"

"It's MY business!" Roger snapped. "I don't have to justify what I do."

"One day you'll dismiss the wrong person unfairly and they'll have you in a tribunal. You two disgust me. It's people like you that mean a lot of people out there don't want to work," Rivers said bluntly.

"No, I don't believe that!" Miles said angrily. "People like Daniel are failures, and they should just accept it."

"Like you? Ever ask yourself why you have no friends?"

"Because I chose it that way."

"Bollocks. Just a case of everyone despises a twat like you that thinks he has the right to think that way."

Roger stepped closer to Rivers. "Get – out – of my shop."

Rivers spat on the floor and walked out.

Superintendent Andrew Palmer sat at his desk eyes ahead of him, dreading DI Burroughs' visit. She came in, a look of pure fury in her eyes.

"Sir, with all due respect what did you let Rivers speak for?" she snapped.

"You win some, you lose some. I put faith in my officers."

"How can you be so blasé? The local rag is going to have a field day. I watched their reporter scribbling like mad when Rivers lost it."

"I'll call our public affairs people. I'll tell them to tell the local paper it'd be bad PR for the community."

"And then guess what?"

"What?"

"DS Rivers – or the former DS Rivers, just decided to verbally assault two people in a hardware store. This time they want him charged."

"Have him talked to and warned away. No more."

"Yes sir. I suspended him. I want a full review that will lead to his dismissal."

"You're taking this far too personally." Palmer told her.

"People blaming their special needs for going off the rails. My boy Ben, he's -"

"Oh, spare me – please." Palmer got up and walked over to the window to look at the traffic. He turned to face her and stared her down.

"You're a fine DI, Elizabeth, but I feel you're not very supportive to your officers when they might be losing their way."

"It's MY way, sir."

"Let me handle Rivers. Goodnight." His tone indicated it was in her interests to leave.

Daniel sat at home watching TV. His phone rang.

"All right, Joe?"

"You all right mate? I'm geared up for tomorrow. Pete's been winding me up. Says if you're found guilty he will blame me and batter me."

Daniel chuckled. "How is everyone?"

"Fine. We appreciate you can't really come out at the moment, it's smarter not to."

"I got karate tomorrow night. Could be my last ever class."

"Don't talk like that. You won't go to prison. You said it yourself you daft wanker. By the way, how's it going so far?"

"As well as it can. My barrister actually went quite easy on Brian, but he's getting others to admit I was not in a good way leading up to the incident. You're my first speaker."

"I'm your first. What an honour."

"Yeah. But seriously, that prosecutor's a bastard, but he's really good."

"I'll make him look a mug."

"I really hope so. I'll see you tomorrow, eh?"

"Yeah, sleep well mate."

THIRTY

Even though it had only been three days into the trial it now felt normal to Daniel to arrive at court to report in, and be taken aside by security to the waiting room. In there were two other men. One middle aged in a shabby suit, who needed a shave. The other was a vicious looking skinhead who looked about Daniel's age.

"Hey. You want something?" The skin head suddenly snapped at Daniel.

"No, sorry if I looked at you wrong."

"Oh, are you being funny now?" the yob snapped.

"Hoag, you be nice now," the head guard said.

"Fuck off! I'm about to go inside for some little bitch boy who couldn't take a slap!" He looked at Daniel again. "And if we end up in the same prison, I'll do you, you little fucker!"

"I doubt this lad will be on the same wing as you. He's looking at a year. You'll get eight – if you're lucky," the guard replied.

"Piss poor reward for admitting what I did!"

"All for the Crown versus D O Steele to court number two," the tannoy announced.

Daniel got up. Two of the seven guards present moved towards him.

"Let's get you away from this unpleasant young man shall we, eh?" one guard smiled.

"Yeah, and fuck your mother too!" Hoag snapped.

As they walked along the corridor Daniel asked, "Who was he?"

"Don't you worry about him. He's getting his come-uppance today," the first guard said.

"He's just some street thug who thinks it's OK to bash people up for any reason. Keep walking," the other guard said.

Daniel was led into the now familiar dock and he sat on his familiar hard-backed chair and looked out. He remembered going on a college trip to a court when he was doing his course, and watching a man looking uncomfortable there. He'd never imagined he would one day sit in the dock. What one guard had said was frightening. He was looking at a year. The jurors were ready. A few looked briefly in his direction. He wondered what they were thinking. Roll on the day when one of them spoke the words that would change his life.

The usual formalities took place as the judge entered.

She said, "Members of the jury, today the defence will present their case. Mr Brooks, if you please."

"Thank you, your honour," Brooks nodded. "Ladies and gentlemen of the jury, good morning – just. I think it's nearly twelve," He let the polite laughs subside.

"There is no denying that the defendant attacked Brian Lever. So why plead not guilty? As I have shown hopefully, Daniel Steele was in a very bad state of mind. Finally he was pushed too far, and he snapped. Certainly, Brian Lever did not deserve to be attacked. Mr Steele had been pushed so far by the store he worked at that he temporarily lost the ability to know right from wrong.

My first witness is, however, a witness of his good character. I call my first witness, Joe McGinty."

Joe entered. He nodded at Daniel who gave him a small smile back, and was then sworn in.

Brooks talked to him and had him tell the jury about Daniel's general behaviour before he worked at Fast Service. And then during the time there leading up to the alleged assault.

Joe told of how Daniel had always had issues, what with the knife attack he had been through. He was good natured, easy going. While he was working at Fast Service his behaviour became more verbally irrational. Openly shouting about social inadequacies, mistreatment in the work place. Joe joked that he had feared his friend was going communist.

The jurors laughed and even Nolan smiled at that remark. But after being sacked he took up his previous activities and he seemed much more relaxed, despite the impending trial. Brooks thanked him and then finished his cross examination.

"Mr Hague you may proceed, if you wish to," Nolan said.

Hague rose and stared hard at Joe. Hague said harshly. "Mr McGinty, you've been unemployed for two years, on disability benefits, you spend most of your time drinking, and you are an alcoholic are you not?"

"Yes, but not a full-on one. I can stand and talk here, can't I?"

"Mr McGinty, an alcoholic you are nonetheless at your own admission."

"I'm here because Daniel felt that I was best suited to deal with you; to wipe that smug smirk off your face," Joe smiled sweetly.

"Mr McGinty," Nolan said sternly.

"No your honour, it's all right," Hague told her. "Yes, certainly a man working would be a little alien to you would it not? You say Mr Steele lost his way because of the shifts he had to do. But I realise you would forget, that is work."

"What, removing someone's right to have a life? Maybe you've no mates, but Daniel has, and he did karate because it gave him self-belief after what he went through. But the boss removed it."

"Sadly, it is just unfortunate..."

Joe leaned forward glaring at him. "Until you're the victim of a traumatic incident, don't you ever pass judgement on how people feel. Daniel needed help and he was denied."

"Which I suppose with your mentality makes it all right to beat up a fifty-seven year-old man?"

"Where I knock about if you pick on someone don't be surprised if you get attacked."

"Mr Lever was doing his job. You'd certainly empathise though wouldn't you? What with losing your job for being insubordinate and showing a clear disrespect for authority?"

"You try slogging it out for peanuts and still getting grief, you posh prick," Joe snarled.

"Your honour, if I may," Brooks stood up. "I feel my learned friend has made his point of discrediting Mr McGinty. But the witness has not denied his past."

"I agree," Hague said. "This witness is a joke in my eyes. Is this really the best character witness the defence can come up with?"

"Mr Hague, kindly refrain from making insulting remarks about the defence. I agree that you have made your point, and I think Mr McGinty will snap if you keep pushing him. Witness is excused."

"Just because of what I am doesn't make my testimony any less true," Joe glared hard at Hague and walked out.

This was to be the longest day. Woods and Brooks had not liked it, but they had to be on a tight schedule. Next Brooks called in Jimmy Hatton. Hatton said that Daniel was not the most efficient of workers, but was a decent guy. And with the right people he did put the effort in. He said that in his opinion Brian Lever was just an opinionated bully, who had gotten people dismissed in the past for having done something wrong, yes, but his real reason was out of spite.

Hague could do little except point out that Hatton was just doing this out of spite, as he and Lever openly despised each other.

Jack Anson was next. He told how he was given a hard time, how Daniel was a good friend. Hague retaliated by saying that while there was no denying his special needs, he did have a severe authority problem and he never had told Lever of his special needs, so why would Lever not consider him to be lazy? Wayne Isaacs testimony was just that Daniel was a good, caring man. Hague decided not to cross examine him.

After that Nolan announced an hour's recess. Daniel watched the court clear. Woods approached him.

"Are you ready?" he asked.

"I think I am. How do you reckon Hague is going to be?"

"Aggressive, tough, ruthless. Just remember he will try his hardest to beat his answers out of you. Whatever you do, don't get worked up. That's when I've seen defendants lose or come close to losing the case."

"Would you say either side is winning?"

"It's pretty close. A lot of it will come down to Dr McLeish's testimony."

"After me, what then?"

"End of court. Tomorrow, Hague and Brooks will make the closing arguments. Then it's in the hands of the jury."

Daniel shook his head. "I just can't believe I could be in prison in two days' time."

Woods smiled gently. "Don't think about it."

Then they heard Joe say. "Is Daniel here?"

Woods nodded. "Here, you can talk now."

Daniel was aware of the guards standing nearer. Joe faced him.

"How'd I do mate?" Joe asked.

"You did fine. Hague tried to discredit you, but that doesn't make your testimony any less true."

"No. You feel like a beer?"

"I'd love to. But I don't think they want me to leave yet. I'll come out later though." Daniel sighed. "It could be my last night as a free man."

It still didn't feel real though.

An hour later, Dr McLeish stood in the witness stand. Daniel had heard some irritated murmurs from Brian's side about how this was so pointless.

Brooks went through McLeish's credentials with him, to show the jury that he was fully qualified to speak on Daniel's behalf.

"Dr McLeish, you were Mr Steele's psychologist before he went to work at Fast Service, is that right?"

"Yes, it is."

"Please tell us the periods of time you treated him."

"Of course. I started treating him before he had his job in the hardware store. And when he worked at the supermarket beforehand."

"Why did he leave the supermarket?"

"He needed a break. He had developed obsessive anxiety which made it hard for him to do his job."

"Obsessive: like obsessive compulsive disorder?"

"Precisely. He feared that if he did not do things in a certain way, family members would suffer terrible fates."

"You believe this was associated with the knife attack?"

"Yes, I do. Obsessive compulsive disorder and post-traumatic stress disorder are commonly linked. The OCD is often the minds way of shielding the individual from the real traumas they are going through. It is certainly not a pleasant way though.

"I felt it a bit extreme him leaving his job, but I could appreciate why he did it. He was ambitious and wanted to succeed, and felt he would not do so there. I treated him for the five weeks he was unemployed. I felt we were making progress. He took on the hardware store job. He thought it was relaxing at first.

"But they dismissed him for his learning difficulties, and for being in therapy."

"Your Honour," Hague interrupted. "If I may, that is opinion, not fact. It is illegal to discriminate for both those issues mentioned."

"It is," McLeish said. "I had a feeling that would be said. So I brought a copy of their letter of notification."

Daniel smiled. Genius doc, he thought, watching McLeish pull out and hand a sheet of paper to Woods, who read it out loud.

"Yes, the letter, signed by Roger Major, the owner of Major's Hardware states that Daniel Steele was found to be hard working and willing. Sadly, it was felt he did not show enough initiative." Brooks looked at Nolan.

He read, "'Also, by going on other things that should have been mentioned at the interview we must make the unfortunate decision that we cannot offer you a permanent place.' It ends with giving four weeks' notice."

"Opinion this may be, but it sounds as if they were covering their backs against a potential tribunal." Brooks said.

"I'd agree," McLeish said. "A lot of my patients starting new jobs fear telling the employer for fear of discrimination. And as proved there, the employer can quite easily cover their backs by writing drivel."

"That alone would be upsetting," Brooks said. "But how was Mr Steele after that?"

"He felt that he could never succeed in anything. He had been victimised also in the supermarket for his problems, by a group of bullies."

"And then he ended up at Fast Service. You had your last meeting with him the week before he started."

"Yes, he thought this was a good opportunity, he said it might be hard to get any therapy for the first few weeks, that as a new starter he would be stuck with bad hours. So after four weeks I posted an appointment. He phoned me and said the manager had been very uncooperative; demanding to know why it wasn't mentioned at the interview that he would need to go to therapy and saying it was up to him to sort it out in his own time. The first appointment he had an afternoon to night shift when it took place.

"I gave him an earlier appointment two weeks later, but he phoned me up and said his shift that day meant he would not be able to make it again. He said that he felt it was not worth continuing."

"And when you met with him and discussed the incident. What are your opinions of his state of mind?"

"He had been victimised for his special needs. He had not been able to continue karate, which gave him his self-confidence, having been through that knife assault. He was also denied help because it was 'inconvenient'."

"Did he speak about Brian Lever?"

"Yes he did. He said how that man was always giving him glares and subtly putting him down. On his case about being slow to learn, and making it clear that he did not care about his problems."

"So the big question. In your professional opinion, what was Daniel Steele's state of mind at the time of the assault?"

"The previous night, talking to his friend who was a rape victim -"

"Said she was a rape victim your honour. The men were all cleared," Hague leapt in.

"Thank you Mr Hague. The doctor is talking about the defendant's state of mind here," Nolan said curtly.

"If I may," McLeish gave Hague a look. "That alone put him in a bad mood, but on its own, not an unstable one. However, like many PTSD sufferers, he was in a fragile state. All the time he was suffering at that store his mind became more fragile.

"Finally, that day he had had enough. He was under a heavy burden of mental trauma and frustration to the point that at that moment in time he was unaware of his actions and the consequences. In fact just before the attack he had yelled that there were far worse things in this world. To Mr Steele with all the things he had seen and heard it defied belief that he was being given a hard time over something as trivial as basic store work. He came under a delusion that there was no wrong in what he did, until shortly after, when it hit him."

"So to simplify it, legally insane. Temporarily insane," Brooks said. "Is he of any further threat to the public in your opinion?"

"Obviously he could no longer have me treat him as I was speaking on his behalf today. He has been seeing Dr Sue Williams and in her opinion, as long as he remains in treatment for the near future he is of no threat."

Brooks smiled broadly at the jury. "We've seen witnesses on both sides, but this is the first one to be able to speak professionally," He turned to Nolan. "I have no further questions your honour. Thank you very much, Dr McLeish."

"Mr Hague," Nolan said.

Hague shot right up, a furious expression on his face. "You can imagine doctor, how I find it personally offensive that you can use this to justify assault on Mr Lever."

"Of course I can. But you must also see I am representing a former patient of mine who could not attend therapy as a result of a store manager."

"Could he not have done a morning appointment?"

"Maybe, but the lack of support and the changing shifts made him give up."

"As he never declared his needs at the interview the defendant has only himself to blame."

"It is a person's legal right to get help."

"As it is Mr Lever's legal right to see justice done, but you feel he deserved it apparently. Dr McLeish, are you sure that Mr Steele was not just in a drunken rage? A blood sample showed he had a high level of alcohol in his blood stream."

"But he was not drunk at the time of the assault."

Hague smiled. "Really? So why did three witnesses to the assault say he was high when he came in? Also, a level of alcohol in your blood stream can still make you behave irrationally can it not?"

McLeish fidgeted uncomfortably. "Yes it can. But I've told you -"

"Are you a court appointed psychologist?" Hague cut in.

"No."

"But this is not your first time speaking on a client's behalf is it?"

"No, I've spoken for twelve previously."

"Yes, and five were found guilty were they not?"

"Two of them had plead guilty!" McLeish said stunned.

"You have refused to speak on behalf of eight people. Is that correct doctor? These people you felt were sane at the time of the offence?"

"Yes, I did," McLeish looked angry.

"Three of them were found not guilty were they not?"

"As you said, I'm not a court appointed psychologist."

"Eight times, out of twenty you were wrong, that's a very bad ratio."

"According to people who are not trained in the field of psychology."

"So the times you won, they could have been wrong are you saying?"

McLeish didn't answer.

Hague continued, "I'm very curious about Mr Steele being denied therapy."

"How so?"

"Well, could he not as I have already said, have got a morning appointment?"

McLeish looked stunned. "He shouldn't have had to!"

"But he still could have, yes?"

"Yes, but it would have been harder, what with other patients -"

"Thank you doctor, you've answered my question. So really, the defendant has only himself to blame for not getting treatment, I think."

"He was also denied the opportunity to go to karate and see his friends regularly which would have helped to keep his mood stable."

"It's an unfortunate fact of life. It can't be used to justify what he did. I have no further questions." Hague sat down.

"You are excused, Dr McLeish," Nolan said.

McLeish gave Hague a brutal look and left.

Watching, Daniel breathed deeply. Him now. Brooks rose and said, "I call the defendant, Daniel Steele," Daniel was escorted through the court to the witness stand. Brooks faced Daniel. Brooks smiled, as Daniel took the oath. Brooks then spoke "Mr Steele, the assault itself. How well do you recall what happened?"

"I don't. It was over so quick. It was like it was someone else and not me."

"I see. Did you feel any remorse?"

"I was aware it was wrong what I had done. I felt I should have, but I couldn't feel bad. The man was a bully. He was always putting me down. Virtually since I had started."

"How do you mean?"

"He always walked around with an angry look on his face. I found it very off-putting. I tried to talk to him when I was new, and he was very abrupt, made it clear he disliked me. When he was pushing stock cages in, I was the only one who used to help him to pull them over the step. He never acknowledged it.

"As time went on he would stomp through me, and I'd have to jump aside quickly to get out of his way."

"You failed one time, is that right?"

Daniel nodded. "He had a go at me, like it was my fault. Also he would snap out my name and expect me to come running."

"What happened when you told him you had problems learning?"

"He said he didn't believe me. That I should not lie!"

"What is the point in this, your Honour?" Hague demanded.

Brooks looked angrier than Daniel had ever seen him. He stopped to calm himself. "Could my learned FRIEND not have the courtesy of patience? I feel these facts are relevant Hour honour. If you do not, please say and I will move along!"

Nolan nodded. "Proceed," she said.

"Thank you, your Honour," Brooks said. "You spoke to him about how unhappy you were with your hours didn't you?"

"Yes, I did. He told me if I didn't like it – quit. I tried to say how I felt, and he just repeated what he had said."

"And he victimised others to in your opinion."

"That's not right your Honour!" Hague snapped.

"In Mr Steele's opinion," Brooks riposted.

"Proceed," Nolan said.

Hague didn't look worried, what was he thinking? Daniel thought. "It was my understanding he did, yes."

"Karate was very therapeutic to you wasn't it? Given the knife attack," Brooks asked.

"It gave me self-belief, it made me less paranoid. It made me calmer."

"The shifts you did denied you it. Had you spoken to Mark Edmunds at the interview about it?"

"Yeah," he said. "Saturday mornings he'd need me, but he'd give me Wednesday off. After three weeks that changed. When I protested he claimed there was nothing he could do, just like with me doing every weekend morning."

"And having a social life must have been hard?"

"It was. I mean, I still went out most weekend nights, but I had to get up a few hours later."

"Did you feel drunk on the morning you attacked Brian Lever?"

"Tipsy maybe."

"Finally you were just pushed over the edge and – BANG! You snapped."

"Yes. Something just went. I didn't feel like me for that minute."

"What with the knife attack, the victimisation you had had in the past, being denied what kept you calmer. Finally your mind went – and you did what you did."

"I think at that moment in time I just felt all the things that upset me and he was so harsh – it just happened."

Brooks faced the jury. "This man went through a horrendous hostage knife attack when three thugs held him and badly slashed him with a knife." He faced Nolan and picked up a brown envelope.

"I have copies of the photographs taken as evidence, as well as the CPS file. Shall I show the jury?"

Hague stood. "I object to this as I feel this bears no relevance."

Nolan looked from Brooks to Hague and then to the jury. "I will need to examine this and hear the reasons for why I should or should not allow it. Members of the jury, I will call a half hour recess."

Half an hour later Daniel sat in the dock, watching the grim faced judge take her seat. Neither Woods, Brooks nor Hague showed any emotion.

Nolan spoke. "Upon discussion with the parties concerned I have decided to allow this. Please proceed, Mr Brooks"

"Thank you, your Honour," Brooks said. He showed the jury the pictures and talked in detail of the incident before concluding by stating that this incident would most certainly cause severe trauma and damage to a person's state of mind. Then he said "I think that's all. Thank you Mr Steele." He smiled and sat down.

"Mr Hague," Nolan said.

Hague stood. "That's a good sob story Mr Steele. Are you sure you're not trying to guilt trip the jury into finding you innocent?"

"I don't want to be found guilty. But what I said is true."

"Indeed it is. That you were denied certain aspects of life, but sadly it happens to us all."

"It made me feel lousy."

"And that justifies attacking a man who is almost an OAP, does it?"

"No, but I just lost it!"

"Well, if that is a reason for acquittal then we might as well let nearly every person in prison free mightn't we?"

"Look, I'm not as good with vocab as you are. What I want to say is, I couldn't focus, or think that morning. All I could think of was what Michelle went through."

"She lied. The men were found not guilty," Hague chided.

"Your Honour!" Brooks shot up. "This is Mr Steele's opinion and my learned friend knows it. That's a blatant attempt at provocation!"

"Sustained. Don't even think about going there, Mr Hague," Nolan ordered.

"Very good your honour, but I am only stating facts," Hague had a smirk on his face. Daniel felt he would love to leap over and knock it off him. "So Mr Steele, you were upset, does that make it all right to do what you did?"

"No. It was all the things piling up higher and higher. I couldn't think, I just snapped!" Daniel glared at Hague. "You think I was just drunk, don't you Hague?"

"Well, I'll tell you what I think shall I?"

"Please do."

"You hated your work place, hated the unfair hours you had to do, hated what you had been through, being victimised for dyspraxia, the knife attack, the OCD, not being able to do karate, your social life being impaired. Am I right?"

"Yes, you are."

"Lastly, you hated Brian Lever. The man you felt picked on you unfairly."

"I think hate's a strong word, I certainly disliked him."

"All those things you hated, you saw in him. He was the object of your hatred, your fury, your anger at how your life had gone, and you decided to attack him, to exorcise the rage in you; to take it out on someone."

Daniel felt a cold fear grip him. He shook his head desperately. But part of him thought Hague could be right. Was that what it boiled down to? Had he lashed out because of how he felt about his life? Had he?

"Am I correct?" Hague smiled, almost benignly at him. Daniel shook his head again desperately. "I think I've touched a nerve. It occurs to me that you've genuinely believed all this time that you were temporarily insane."

"No, no," Daniel gasped.

"I think that's how you justified what you did to yourself isn't it?" Hague spoke seemingly kindly now. "Because you knew it was wrong. Come on, admit it, and make things easier on yourself." Behind Daniel the two guards moved close.

Daniel forced himself to look up. "It would make sense wouldn't it? But you're wrong. I think there is guilt in me, and that's why I hesitated just now."

"I don't think so, I don't think the jury will either." Hague smiled.

"Your Honour -" Brooks started.

"No need Mr Brooks, I'm finished." Hague waved dismissively as he turned away from Daniel.

Exhausted, Daniel collapsed into his chair.

After adjournment Hague stood with Partt, Brian and his wife.

"I think they're on the ropes now," Partt said smiling. "It came down to Steele, George and you got him."

"So tomorrow is the sum ups, and maybe verdict?" Brian asked.

"All being well the jury will reach a verdict after sum ups, but it often takes longer." Hague explained. "I guarantee you a few jurors will buy the sob story and will need, er, persuasion."

"Remind them of my age!" Brian snapped at Hague.

Hague smiled. "I intend to."

A short chunky middle aged woman approached them. "Cora Denham, Mansford Chronicle. If you have any comments Mr Lever, I'll be happy to hear them after the verdict." She smiled.

"He certainly will!" Mrs Lever said angrily.

As Cora left, Joe suddenly appeared and strode over. His eyes stared daggers at Brian.

"Who's the little man with short arse syndrome?" he demanded. "Hope you're fucking happy you twat. My mate could be about to go to prison because of you! He never did anything wrong to anyone you know?"

"You lot are sad pathetic specimens!" Brian said furiously. "Get away from me,"

"Go fuck yourself," Joe growled.

Two security men hurried over. Joe just shook his head. "A man with no mates. What a sad life you have had," He shook his head and walked away before he could be escorted.

Woods and Brooks sat with Daniel.

"You saved it at the end, I was really impressed," Woods said.

"I thought I'd screwed up," Daniel replied.

"No, why do you think Hague backed off that quick?" Brooks smiled.

"Hague surprised us all. We were expecting an aggressive cross examination; not what he did," Woods told him.

"How do you think we did?" Daniel smiled nervously, dreading the reply.

"It is so hard to say," Woods told him. "But go out tonight, try and relax as best you can and we'll see you half ten tomorrow morning."

"Be good Daniel," Brooks smiled. He ushered Daniel out.

Then after a minute Woods said, "He's going to be found guilty isn't he, Gary?"

"I don't know, Robert. Let's prepare our summing up."

THIRTY-ONE

Rivers arrived at the police station to collect his personal possessions. Warren Hampson smirked at him as he entered the CID room.

"Always knew you'd fuck up," he sneered.

Rivers walked on.

"That's it, walk away," Hampson continued.

Walker said to Rivers, "I'm sorry about the incident, but I was just so stunned at you. You taught me so much," he told the gaunt-looking Rivers.

"It's ok." Rivers said. "I better get moving. I can't face seeing the DI."

"Smart move," Walker smiled. "She is seething. Roger Major and Miles Booth have both lodged a complaint against you."

Rivers nodded and patted Walker's shoulder.

"I know, I had uniform come to my house and caution me last night,"

"You'll be back shortly sarge," Spears said as Rivers walked out.

"Here's hoping," Walker added.

"That the stupid bastard won't come back," Hampson sniggered.

"Just shut up for once!" Spears growled.

Hampson got up and walked over to where Spears sat. "I'm just saying is all. Stupid sentimental bastard. That's also Sergeant to you. Unlike that idiot now."

Spears leapt up and grabbed Hampson by the scruff and slammed him back into a desk and then wrestled him so he lay on it.

"Mike Rivers is a better police officer than you'll ever be you smug fuck. He got where he got by seeing an investigation as helping a victim, not as a promotional opportunity like you, you selfish bastard."

"You'll be following him when I tell the DI," Hampson gasped.

Walker came over. "No, he won't. If you say anything we'll say you threw the first punch."

Spears was surprised. It was unlike Walker. Spears let the gasping Hampson go. Walker led Spears to a corner.

"I didn't expect that from you," Spears said.

"All right, I hate Hampson for one, and two, Rivers, I sort of feel we owe it to him," Walker replied to Spears.

"Yeah, that was random. Evan's such a thick bastard guys," Joe said in the Silver Seal that evening.

"Meaning what?" Rees asked.

"Ricky's video has me saying I'm like a paedo fag or something. I told Evan and he said, "I didn't realise you were like that Joe'," Joe cracked.

"You remember I used to do boxing and I played rugby at school," Evan shot back.

"And you played with yourself," Pete cracked.

"Evan, don't give me that stare, you're trying to impersonate Pete," Joe smiled.

"Let me get this straight, are you saying Evan's thick?" Daniel asked innocently.

"Yes, I am," Joe grinned. "You did boxing, eh?" Evan nodded. "Yeah, making them maybe, and the only time you played rugby was when you were nineteen and the opposition was twelve." Laughs came up.

"That's it. I've had enough." Evan had to smile.

He chased Joe who ran out the back door. The group followed laughing as Evan chased Joe around the beer garden. After a minute Evan grabbed him in a head lock. Ricky and Matt jogged over. Ricky stuck his shoe out.

"Lick that for me," he laughed.

"Fuck that, I'm going to make him lick the ground." Evan replied.

"Come on Evan, enough eh?" Matt smiled.

"What? We're messing about. How about the time you thumped him for being racist?" He let Joe go.

"That was a year ago and we were both hammered." Matt replied.

Standing next to Pete, Daniel said, "I'll miss this if I go inside."

"Yeah, but you won't," Pete said. "Let's get some shots guys."

Pete bought them all a shot of whisky. "Here's to Daniel getting off tomorrow." He lifted his glass high.

"Here, here," they shouted back and then necked them. Daniel felt the happiest he had in a long time. These were his friends.

At eight am his alarm went off. Daniel had slept well. Sitting up in bed to turn it off he was only too aware this could be the last night he slept there in a long time. One year could have him serving a long time inside he thought. He ate breakfast. His parents spoke little and the car ride was deathly silent except for his parents having a brief sharp row about a driving incident.

They were clearly terrified. Daniel tried to force himself to be as calm as he could. How many people were baying for him to be sent down? He thought about all the time since then. Had he been insane at the time? Now he doubted it. But it was too late now. He still felt no remorse. Brian Lever was a nasty bully. Daniel had not been the only one the sadistic bastard had picked on.

His brother and sister had arrived first and met him and his parents. Then Daniel was taken into the waiting room for the last time, he hoped. Woods had warned him juries sometimes took a long time to reach a verdict. Daniel hoped not. Even if he was found guilty, he wanted it all over. One woman and a man sat in there with seven guards. Daniel nervously sipped his vending machine coffee.

"Douggie Hoag got ten years by the way," a guard told him.

"Sorry?"

"That man who gobbed off at you. He got ten years for the assault, but he had that much tagged on as they proved he'd intimidated many victims and was a clear menace to society," the head guard explained. "All three of us had to hold him back. He hurled insults at the judge, the prosecutor, us, even his own defence." The guard shook his head.

"All for The Crown versus D O Steele to Court number two," the tannoy announced.

Two guards led him to the court room. He entered, taking a deep breath as he did so. He walked to his chair and sat down.

The usual formalities were gone through. Nolan stated that it was time for the closing arguments, then looked sternly at Hague, before saying,

"Mr Hague, if you please."

"Thank you, your Honour," Hague said. "Good morning," he said to the jury. "This has been an interesting case. It holds in the balance, a young man's life and I don't expect your verdict to be an easy one.

"You must decide who you believe, me or the defence. In my honest opinion, they are using a sob story, nothing more. Some of you may think that Brian Lever is an unpleasant person; you may indeed have worked with people like him. So you may empathise with the defendant. But you cannot JUSTIFY assault. Brian Lever will be 58 in July. Nearly an OAP. And Daniel Steele attacked him for being a demanding boss. At least one punch a karate one. Can Mr Lever be faulted for being demanding of a high standard? Even Steele believed until yesterday, he was innocent. He's had his defence, his psychologist tell him he was mentally unhinged. A psychologist, I might add who has been proven wrong on many occasions.

"Steele's reaction alone to my questions yesterday should prove his guilt. He says he was denied his life. That is wrong, but not justification for what he did. He was denied therapy for his problems. No he was not, it was an inconvenience, but he could have quite easily re-scheduled to week day mornings. He is his own worst enemy, and now I hope you will make the right decision and find him guilty. Brian Lever deserves justice.

"We have the right to a fair and SAFE working environment. Steele violated that, perhaps under the influence of his friends, several of whom have assault convictions. Perhaps under the influence of alcohol, which we know he was under. May I remind you that a blood test showed a level of alcohol in his blood? And I don't have to tell you that can make some people violent. Not an unstable mind as his defence claim.

"Members of the jury, I thank you. You have complimented me with your patience throughout the trial. On that note, the Crown rests its case," Hague turned to smile in the direction of the public gallery.

Woods and Brooks were whispering to each other. Nolan interrupted. "Mr Brooks, you may proceed."

"Thank you, your honour." Brooks stood and faced the jury. He sighed hard. "Daniel Steele has suffered enough in his life. He has been victimised for his severe learning disability, made to feel useless. He has been the victim of a traumatic knife attack. So please consider that his social life and karate were important to his state of mind. These things that give his life meaning are removed. He is victimised by the alleged victim, a man who is a bully without even realising it at his own admission, because understandably Mr Lever is used to things in a whole different way.

"But it is proven by doctors that dyspraxia exists. Brian Lever has no medical training, no right to claim that it does not exist. He has had so many complaints made, and yet he claims he's hard but fair. Eleven known complaints! What does that say?

"Now members of the jury, I am not saying he deserved to be attacked. I am saying it was Mr Lever who finally pushed Daniel Steele that little bit too far.

"Mr Steele had been pushed by superiors who did not care that he put the graft in, just that he could not understand quickly enough. How would that make you feel? Plus he carried the permanent trauma of the knife attack that would leave anyone's mind seriously disturbed. Dr McLeish states that, as well as the fact that he is not a public threat.

"Now as my learned friend points out, Dr Mcleish has been wrong in court eight times out of twenty. But he's been right twelve of those times and I feel he is better qualified to speak than any of us. And he says Daniel Steele was in poor mental health. Rest assured if he walks free from here, he will still be under conditions such as continuing therapy. He will not be allowed to approach Brian Lever. Let me remove any nagging doubts from your mind. On that note I rest my case."

Nolan spoke to the jurors, instructing them in their thinking. She then dismissed them to reach a verdict.

Three hours later, Daniel sat in the waiting room listening to music on his iPod play. He had eaten a McDonald's meal that his parents had bought him. The jurors had been hard to read as they had left, but after nearly three hours of deliberating, it was even harder to say what they were concluding.

Walker represented the police at the trial. He approached Brian, his wife and Hague. A young Muslim girl stood with them who Brian was speaking to furiously to.

"You let me down Aisha," he snarled. "Speaking like that!"

"I swore on the Koran to speak the truth. I'm sorry, Brian but I have to be honest."

"Indeed she does," Hague cut in. "Mr Lever, people must say it as they know it. We may not have liked it, but she could not lie."

"How's it holding up?" Walker cut in.

Brian looked like he was close to exploding. "Where's DS Rivers? I hope you sacked him!"

"I can assure you he has been suspended, pending a review," Walker smiled.

"What was he doing in there? Saying those things?"

"I'm afraid as you were just told, people can't lie under oath. Not that I condone what he did."

Brian looked furious and was about to say more when the clerk walked out. "They're ready," he said quietly.

Three and a half hours, Daniel thought. He was suddenly aware of Brooks standing over him. "They're ready Daniel."

Daniel turned his iPod down, and then off. "What's the verdict? Please tell me."

"I don't know it. Come on, son."

Daniel walked along the corridor, for the last time, he thought. All these times, it felt unreal. This time he had four guards. He guessed in case the verdict was guilty and he tried to do something stupid. One opened the door. Daniel breathed deeply and then walked in. He approached his chair and sat down. He looked at the jurors, they betrayed nothing.

"All rise," the clerk announced.

They all stood. Out of the corner of his eye Daniel saw Brian, eyes dead ahead this time.

"Please be seated," Nolan said.

They sat for a few seconds and then Nolan nodded at the clerk.

"Please rise, Mr Steele," the clerk said.

Daniel stood, fighting to stay calm.

Nolan faced the foreman, a middle aged man who looked uncomfortable, like whatever verdict had been reached, he personally disagreed with.

"Have the jury reached a verdict on which you are all agreed?" Nolan asked.

"Yes, your honour we have," the foreman replied.

"Good. On the charge of assault, how do you find the defendant Daniel Steele?"

"Not guilty, not guilty," Daniel willed him to say.

The foreman looked at the ground, and then up to face the judge.

"Guilty."

Daniel collapsed into his chair. The word seemed to thump into his brain. Dimly, he was aware of his mother sobbing, dimly he could hear someone in the public gallery say, "They got it right!"

Then dazedly he could hear the judge speaking to him, "Please remain standing Mr Steele."

One guard put their hands under his arms to lift him, but Daniel shrugged him off. He could see Hague smiling in the direction of the public gallery at who must be Partt and Brian. Daniel gripped the rail of the dock tight, dreading the words to follow.

"Daniel Steele, you have been found guilty of assault, and in my opinion, rightly so. Maybe you genuinely believed that you were pushed over the edge to the point you could claim ill mental health. However the reality is you had just had enough. That is why you lashed out. You had so much resentment in you, you had to do it."

Judge Nolan leant back. Daniel just wanted her to say the sentence. "Mr Hague has requested you be given a hard sentence to set an example," Daniel had to hold himself up. It would be a year. "But I will take into consideration, your previous good character. This is your first offence.

"The way you have been treated in the world of work, made to feel worthless. That you do suffer from trauma. It has been proved that Mr Lever did treat you badly along with others, however, it does not justify your attack.

"It is with all this in mind that I pass the custodial sentence of twelve months," She hesitated letting it sink in. Before she spoke again. "But I will suspend it for twelve months."

Daniel looked stunned at Woods who grinned as if to say, 'Yeah, you heard right.' Now it was his side's turn to give relieved gasps, and the public gallery sides turn to sound angry.

"Order," Nolan said sharply. Silence descended. "As this sentence is suspended you will adhere to certain rules, if you violate them it will be revoked.

"If you are found guilty of another criminal act you will receive the new sentence plus what is left of the suspended sentence. You will not enter the Fast Service C-store in Mansford, or stand directly outside it. You are banned from directly approaching Brian Lever. You are to continue attending therapy until such a time as you are seen to have recovered and I will allow you to continue karate, as it appears to calm you. Do you accept my conditions?"

"Yes, your honour!" Daniel said happily. He wanted to thank her, but felt it inappropriate.

"That is all. Court is adjourned. My thanks to the jurors," she said.

"All rise," the clerk said loudly.

They all stood. Daniel watched the jurors filter out. He could hear the sounds of people leaving. Woods then approached Daniel.

"Think you can keep out of mischief for the next year?" He smiled at Daniel.

"I think so. Are the press outside?"

"Don't flatter yourself, you're not that big a story, you know," Woods laughed.

Daniel laughed too. "But I do now have a criminal conviction," he said, sadly.

"Yeah, but at least you're walking a free man. I mean, you could have been being loaded into a prison van now."

"That's true. How will the media respond to all this?"

"To be blunt, you'll be the bad guy. Another product of our 'soft' legal system. But it'll cool off."

"Couldn't I tell my side? To a reporter I mean?"

Woods sighed. "This isn't Hollywood, Daniel. No fairy tale endings. To the local rag you'll be the bad guy. I saw The Chronicle rep scarper pretty quickly after court finished. No doubt after your friend Brian."

"To listen to him rant? I spent all that time at Fast Service listening to it. Every Sunday morning. Do you realise I only worked one day a week with him? Occasionally, two on the rare occasion someone was away and I was rota-ed to fill in. That place almost ruined me."

"You're out now, and maybe your probation officer might be able to fix employment up for you."

"Yeah, maybe. Thanks for all you did."

Outside Joe and Ricky watched Brian Lever pose for a photograph. A very angry look on his face.

They listened to him say loudly: "What a fiasco that that man can walk free from here after what he did, and it just proves that there is no protection in the work place for people in authority."

"What, in my job there's none for the rank and filers," Ricky said stunned. "Some of the managers there just tell us to quit if we complain and if not to shut up."

"I guess it can work both ways," Joe mused. "For Daniel's sake I'm glad it has."

"Do you think he should have been found guilty?"

"Pete reckoned he would, but he felt it worth a try to get off. Here he comes."

Daniel walked slightly ahead of his parents, Woods followed.

A camera snapped a picture of him.

Mrs Lever yelled "You horrible little sod! Don't you feel ashamed of what you did? You should be on your way to prison now!"

Mr Steele took Daniel's arm and guided him away.

"Maybe your husband shouldn't be bullying people for disabilities!" Mrs Steele shouted.

Woods gently took her by the arm. "Don't give them the satisfaction," he whispered.

For Daniel the drive home seemed unreal. That he was going home and not to prison. The fact that he had a criminal record now was something he did not consider.

They got back to the house.

"Head in, Daniel. We knew you wouldn't be sent down," Mr Steele smiled.

They got back in and Daniel walked into his bedroom. He'd been uncertain he'd be seeing it again for a long time this morning.

"Just remember Daniel, you're on license for a year," Mrs Steele said suddenly.

"Thanks mum. I haven't." He smiled.

"I'm just saying, you don't want to get in any trouble," she pressed.

"No, I won't."

"I just feel it worth mentioning is all."

"Sarah," Mr Steele said, "let him enjoy the moment."

She nodded and walked away. Daniel walked around his room. "I did it," he said. "I did it. I DID IT!"

THIRTY-TWO

Daniel bought a copy of the Chronicle the next morning. To his relief his story was not front page. After buying it he sat down on a bench and found it on page four. To the left side of the article was a picture of him nervously standing in the dock. To the right was a picture of Brian looking angry. The article read:

SUPERVISOR'S DISGUST AT LENIENT SENTENCE HANDED OUT TO HIS ATTACKER

Mr Brian Lever, a supervisor at the local Fast Service convenience store slammed what he felt was a shockingly lenient sentence on the man who attacked him at work.

Former colleague, Daniel Steele had brutally lashed out at him when Mr Lever had told him off about a mistake he had made.

Steele, 24 showed no remorse during the trial, having pleaded not guilty through being mentally unstable, as was testified to by Dr McLeish, his psychologist. The jury found Mr Steele guilty.

George Hague, prosecuting had stated that Steele had probably believed he was mentally unstable as a way of justifying what he had done, but that really he was merely angry at what he felt was unfair treatment he had received, in that he was given only unsocial hour shifts.

Judge Abigail Nolan said there could be no justification for Steele's actions and sentenced him to one year, but suspended it on the grounds that Steele had been through traumatic experiences, for which the job had denied him the appropriate treatment.

Mr Lever raged that the sentence showed how little protection those in authority were given. He said, in his opinion, people like Steele should appreciate what they had and not hide behind 'unfair treatment'.

"The door is there if they don't like how things are," he stated.

Jean Hendry, who has worked at the store for two years said, "We feel bad for Brian. He is a very dedicated man to getting the job done, and he doesn't suffer fools gladly. We all feel he deserved justice for the attack that was most certainly unprovoked."

At home Rivers sat reading the same article. He felt sickened by Brian's comment about 'appreciating what they had'. It was that sort of naivety that he had suffered in his youth. He looked hard at the picture of Brian Lever and drove his fist into it.

Brian went into the store that day. He saw Lesley Griffin, a colleague.

"We're all sorry about the sentence," she said. "He should have got a year – inside."

"He certainly should" Brian said.

Ken Dyker, the relief manager came over. "Brian, how are you?" he asked quickly.

Brian disliked him and as always with people he disliked, made no effort to hide it.

"Fine," he said, bluntly.

"He should have been sent to prison," Dyker continued. "I think so."

"Oh, right," Brian said disinterestedly.

Ken smiled and walked on. As Brian came to the way in/out, Jimmy Hatton approached him.

"Too bad about Daniel, eh," he smirked.

"It made your day, didn't it?" Brian's temper flared.

Jimmy leaned in closer. "Anything that makes a nasty bastard like you unhappy cheers me up," he sneered, and walked away, leaving Brian seething.

Miles Booth always went home for lunch. He had read the article and was disgusted that Steele had walked free. He was walking back along a quiet road where there was usually little or no traffic. He enjoyed it. It was tranquil. He saw another man and recognised him as that policeman he had made a complaint against, what was his name? Riley, no, Rivers that was it.

"Guess you heard about it, eh?" Booth said. "What a shambles our legal system is. Our society."

"Meaning what?" Rivers asked.

"People like Daniel. Who gives a stuff? He's still free and taking my taxes in benefits. It's so wrong."

"Tell me," Rivers said. "Do you feel that way about people who have no self-belief to work, because they have had their self-belief taken away?"

"No, that's no excuse!" Miles snapped.

"So people who for some reason have no self-esteem that's still no excuse. What should they do?"

"Just be forced to deal with it," Miles glared at him. "Think I don't know about you? We had a friend of Brian Lever's in our store saying how you got all sympathetic because you lost the plot when you were younger. Just like Daniel. He won't ever get anywhere – and neither will you."

Rivers suddenly lunged forward and wrestled the terrified Miles into a side alley. Rivers slammed him with hard force into the wall. Miles looked around desperately, but, no one was there. Rivers punched him in the left side of the head, and then again in the belly. The hefty, unfit man went down gasping for air. Rivers stepped back and kicked him in the belly.

"It was people like you that ruined me. Tried to make me think my own life was pointless! Its people like you are so ignorant they put others down to hide what worthless fucks they are!"

Rivers kicked him in the ribs this time. "And it's people like you that have ruined me again."

Rivers stood back breathing deeply. He hated it, but he felt good.

Suddenly he was aware of a powerful grip on his back and he was thrown back into the wall. He looked up and to his surprise saw Pete Redmond standing there.

"What are you doing?" Pete demanded.

"I had to OK?"

"So now you're like us?"

"I'm nothing like you!"

"No? You beat up a man because he pissed you off, the same as I did. Was this about Daniel?"

Rivers looked at him. "Partly. Now I guess I'm prison bound myself."

"Not necessarily," Pete pulled his work knife out. He looked at the cowering Miles Booth. "You, see this knife, do as I say or I'll cut you. Take out your wallet and throw it to me."

Gasping, Miles dug his wallet out, and threw it in Pete's direction. Pete picked it up and read the inside.

"Mr M Booth. You make yourself sound so important," Pete laughed, then his expression grew fierce and he waved the knife at Miles. "This was just a snatch and grab mugging, understand? You report either of us, I'll see to it you suffer – badly. Do you understand me? My brother died of a drug overdose because he was victimised for his special needs, so harming you would be a pleasure. I've been in prison once because I gave a bloke facial surgery when he said special needs types deserved to suffer. You understand me?"

Pete then stood straight, put a hand on Rivers shoulder and turned him around. They walked briskly for ten minutes, before Pete stopped.

"I'll give this money to a charity box," he said.

"Why?" Rivers asked.

"You're the policeman. For one, I don't want to be caught with it and two, I'm no street mugger. I won't profit from what I got there."

"What were you doing here then, eh?" Rivers asked dazed.

"Lucky for you wasn't it? I was working near here and I was taking a walk for my lunch." Pete looked at him. "You still think we're the bad guys don't you?"

"I'm wondering why a formerly clean cut lad like Daniel got involved with you lot," Rivers replied.

Pete shook his head. "There's worse than us aren't there? Some of us have got previous, there's trouble goes with us, sure, like when I ejected that stuck up muppet from The Seal, or the fascists that we know like Alan Saunders and Steve Dodd. But what happens when a good boy like Daniel gets rejected by his own kind. These so-called moral citizens reject him because he's different, because he's got mental health issues. Did you know that some so-called friends of his at the supermarket disowned him because they found out about his trauma issues, and one of them got it into their head that Daniel was going to go schizo and knife them up? Because they're ignorant – and the rest are too, so they follow suit.

"So let me ask you something, what is he going to do? He gets in with us. We treat him right. We don't judge him. I've been around those other lot and they may not have criminal records, but they have no understanding of what's outside of their little world."

"What are you on about?"

"They have no tolerance to what's different. Even the ones who were tearaways as youngsters are now so holier than thou it's sickening."

"Do you want me to understand you lot? Because give up if you do." Rivers said tiredly.

"I think you're scared to. We don't deny what we did or that it was wrong, but reality bites. People like Daniel get in with bad company all the time because the so-called right side of the line makes them feel inadequate."

"That may be, but I have to ask," Rivers smiled thinly. "How is it you sound so well educated?"

Pete had to smile. "Can a building site supervisor not be? Five years inside I did and in those five years I studied and got two qualifications, A-levels in English and in Literature,"

"Look, if Booth does report the attack I won't name you OK?"

"Who'd listen to a whiny little bastard like him?"

Pete watched Rivers walk away.

Later on that day, Daniel went into The Duke for a quiet drink. He sat down and bought a pint. Within five minutes, Laurie shoulder barged him and looked challengingly at him. Daniel ignored him and sipped his drink. Laurie walked away. After another few minutes Daniel was aware of two more men, Stuart and Kyle.

"Oh, look, if it isn't the man who should be in prison." Stuart sneered, sidling up to one side, Kyle took the other.

"Too right, he should," Kyle agreed.

Stuart shoved him in the back. "What's the matter mate? Is it because you know I'll fight back?"

Daniel faced him. "No, we've been through this before, I know you're a pussy faggot, but I also know you'd snitch on me if I so much as push you."

"Yeah, because people who 'snitch' are bad in your mind aren't they?" Kyle said.

Jim the landlord walked over. "Get lost you two," he sighed. "I don't want trouble."

"It's the principle of it," Kyle retorted. "We don't want him here."

"Just go will you." Jim snapped. He watched them walk away. "Listen Daniel, I'm sorry, but I have to ban you."

Daniel looked stunned. "What, why?"

"Too many people are not happy with you being in here. I will have to ask you to leave."

"Yeah, or the police will have to be called. " Laurie smirked.

"Fuck off you arrogant prick," Daniel said through gritted teeth. He turned to Jim. "Can I finish this pint?"

"No," Jim took it off him. "Please don't make this any harder than it has to be."

Daniel sighed and walked out.

THIRTY-THREE

Woods sat in his office and watched the man admitted. Andy Harman his name was. He had been the foreman on the jury. The man who had announced Daniel to be guilty.

"Have a seat," Woods told him and watched Harman, a middle aged medium-sized man who looked nervous, sit down. "I am curious as to why you wanted to see me."

Harman sighed. "I just had to see you. To tell you there were some of us who did not want to find him guilty,"

"Like yourself?"

"Yeah, but it was out of principle, really. Your legal arguments got us to debate as long as we did, but the others were determined."

"I'm glad to hear the defence's arguments carried some weight. Just out of vanity I have to ask, what was the initial vote?"

"Fifty-fifty. The others were swayed pretty quickly though. Legally, I guess he was guilty."

"On paper he was found to be. Chances are that another jury would have voted differently. The judge said to me that she agreed with the verdict, but said myself and Brooks' defence was very good. She felt a weaker defence would never have held things up for so long."

"There's a lot of victimisation goes on out there, that never gets dealt with and we just stand there and watch."

"That's why I felt it necessary Daniel got a good defence." Woods told him.

Daniel felt it risky, but he had to do it. He stood outside Michelle's front door and rang the bell. To his relief she answered.

"Daniel, I don't need any -"

"Please yeah, just a minute, eh? For all we've been through together."

"All right." She folded her arms and gave him a fierce look. "Talk then."

"I guess you know I got off. Guilty but suspended. Look, I'm banned from The Duke now, and that's for good or as long as Jim's landlord anyway. That's the only place we ever saw each other, so we won't really see one another again. I just need to know this, yeah: are we still friends?"

Michelle looked down and then at him. "I can't just abandon what we had. We had some good times I admit. But the side I've seen of you recently..." She shook her head.

"I can't be around you. You know what Kyle means to me and you've threatened him. You must understand, Daniel I care about you and I would still like to know you. But not as before all this happened."

Daniel frowned. "I don't understand."

Michelle stepped forward and took his right hand in hers. "You were a great friend to me and I hope we still can be. But not as we were before. If we see each other I want us to be able to talk to each other, but I can't have you calling me, I don't want to meet up with you."

She let go and stepped back. "I'm sorry Daniel, but now I've seen the other side to you and I don't like it."

Daniel felt his eyes moisten. He put his hands behind his head and licked the inside of his mouth. "Michelle, as a friend I love you so much. Kyle -"

"He will get me telling him to behave himself to you. You know he does what I say."

"Thanks, but I just want what we had."

"Daniel, you know so much about me." She suddenly coughed a sob. "Surely you can understand why I feel this way!" She wiped tears from her eyes. Please go. Don't make this harder. Please!"

Daniel nodded. He turned away and heard the door close. What went through his mind was that it was the first time since the knife attack he had felt his eyes moisten.

THIRTY-FOUR

Adam Chester sat with a nervous smile on his face as he talked to a youth called Ryan Herd, a former colleague at the store. Ryan was a very cocky sort. He had left just before Daniel had started.

"So I reckon Brian got the petrol about that bloke walking," Ryan smirked.

"Yeah," Adam said quietly. "He did."

"I remember my impression of him," Ryan grinned broadly. He bent his knees and made himself much shorter, hardened his face and said in an impression of Brian, "'I'm Brian, I'm a bad tempered man with a major short bloke complex.'"

"Uh, excuse me," a middle-aged woman on the till next to Adam called out. "Some of us like Brian, you know?"

Ryan pulled himself up to his height and picked up his purchases. "He was horrible. I had a mate work here two years ago said if Brian was twenty years younger he'd have punched him out."

Brian suddenly came charging around the corner. Ryan stopped and stared at him.

"Get out now!" Brian thundered.

"Fine by me. The further I am from you the happier I'll be," Ryan chuckled and walked out.

Ken, the manager walked over. "What's all this?" he asked.

"I was just dealing with a problem customer," Brian told him. "He's gone now."

"Good. Brian, I need to talk to you. My office if you don't mind."

Brian frowned and followed Ken into the office. Ken went to the door and closed it. He fixed Brian with a hard stare.

"It's come to my attention that you've been bad mouthing me behind my back."

"I can say what I like."

"Yes, you can." Ken sat down. "So speak. What's your problem?"

"You don't know what you're doing."

"Really? You've been here three years now. How many managers have you had?"

"Three others and I've had problems with them all."

"Yes? I phoned up two of them; Martin Hutchins and Dave Purvis who are still with the company, and guess what? They had problems with you. Said you were a pain in the arse. All the complaints on your record –"

"They've all got attitudes, they were all ignorant."

Ken stood over him. "You really are that arrogant aren't you? It occurs to me that a lot of people speak well of you here, but, what's odd is that maybe only two of them work closely with you."

"You want to watch it. I was a company director. I understand more about business than you ever will!"

"You're not any more though are you? You're a C-store supervisor. I will not tolerate your attitude, your way of thinking any more! I've tried to turn a blind eye, you're a very efficient worker. But I have a store to run, and there are divisions in the staff here. You fall into one side. I want to bring both together. YOU are one of the main causes of the divide. I will not tolerate it any more. Mark Edmunds allowed it. I won't. I show no favouritism. Hours will be changed to be fairer to everyone. They will be on a rotational basis as of two weeks from now. Certain types will not be left to do what they want every week unless they have a bloody good reason. The others will not be left suffering unsociable hours week after week anymore. I'm making changes to increase morale."

"Increase morale? My attitude is if they don't like it to quit! Some of them are lucky to even have a job. They're so useless, especially during a recession."

"Given that that lad who attacked you was demoralised by his hours and treatment you should appreciate my way of thinking. Carly Wells told me how she gave Mark five weeks' notice once about a party she had one Saturday night when he always rota-ed her in. Plenty of notice.

"He just said 'If you can find someone to swap with, fine, otherwise no'. I will not tolerate the favouritism bias that goes on here. Maybe the less motivated will work harder if their hours are fairer."

"This is all wrong, I'm against it. So will others be."

Ken smiled thinly. "If you don't like it – resign." He then walked to the door, opened it and exited leaving Brian seething.

Rivers was at home that morning waiting for his visitor. What made him nervous was that Palmer had just called to say he had to speak with him. Had Miles Booth pressed charges? The door-bell rang. Rivers breathed deeply, walked to the door and answered it. Palmer stood there.

"Sir, come in," Rivers stepped aside.

Palmer nodded and walked in. "You can call me Andrew. This is an informal visit."

Rivers nodded and led Palmer to the living room.

"Nice place, Mike. How long have you lived here for?"

"Four years now."

Palmer nodded. "I'll get to the point. I've got information about your review, informally. You will hear all this at your review."

"Am I to be dismissed?" Rivers asked, dreading the answer.

"No. But you'll be out of CID. You're to be put in uniform. Also demoted to constable."

Rivers stared at the floor. "Is that for good?"

"No. You're going to be put on a psychiatric programme for a while. When that is done, you'll be reviewed on a regular basis to see if you're fit to retain your original status. It's not what you wanted to hear, but it's better than dismissal. What you did was wrong."

"I spoke the truth. Sir – Andrew, the prejudice out there -"

"You have to see both points of view here."

"What?"

"Look me in the eyes and tell me you'd be so tolerant if it weren't for your difficulty."

"I don't know what I'd be like."

"Exactly. It's frustrating dealing with people who you have to repeatedly explain things to, I'm sorry, but that's a fact. You have to realise people have businesses to run and they can't keep looking after people."

"You aren't like that."

"No, I go by what I see in dedication, but that's a thing our profession allows. Most employment can't. It's realistic, and believe me I still think the bullies out there who pick on people with disabilities deserve a hiding if they get one for it. But when it comes to working close up with people with those problems it can get very frustrating."

"It was like Steele's brief said to Brian Lever in court, 'What should happen to people with special needs?' He couldn't answer. Someone told me about it the day I was in court. I think it was the reporter. They felt that Lever was being bullied by the defence, but I would have liked to know his answer.

"Do you realise Andrew, that when people like me and Daniel Steele get what we're doing, we're as good as anyone else. But we're just not given the chance a lot of the time. I don't know if you remember Scott McKenzie, that homeless junkie we used to keep nicking for this, that and the other?"

"No, I don't."

"One time we'd nicked him for going into a pub and harassing people. He was trying to sit with groups of people and get them to buy him drinks. The landlord phoned us up and had him nicked for his own safety, before someone did for him.

"I had a one to one talk with him. Asked him why he was like this. He said to me 'I'm thirty-eight as of yesterday. No one cares. I used to be an honest hard working bloke until I got so much shit at work I just thought 'fuck it!' My family disowned me and I can be a bastard to anyone who tries to help me because I don't feel I deserve any better!' A year later he died of a heroin overdose.

"I realise that could have been me. I almost went down that route."

Palmer looked at him. "It's a tough dilemma. I don't think there's any easy solution or answer."

THIRTY-FIVE

Adam walked along the high street.

"Hey, Adam." He heard, and turned to see Daniel.

"Are you allowed here?" Adam asked nervously.

"I'm not allowed in the store, but I can walk the high street for fuck's sake, as long as I stay away from the store entrance," Daniel smiled.

"I mean, talk to me, or anyone else working there?"

"I can't approach Brian, not that I'd want to."

"Maybe to apologise?"

"I don't feel remorse for it, I'd like to tell you different, but I won't lie. Don't start what you can't finish, the guy was a bully. You feel like a pint?"

Adam shifted uncomfortably. "OK."

"I'm not going to thump you." Daniel told him. "Don't be afraid, I'm not some random thug, you know that, come on. I'll buy you a drink."

Daniel took him into The Cat's Whiskers and bought them both a drink. They sat down.

"I got me a new job." Daniel smiled. "My mate Rees phoned me up last night. It's a factory hand job, not much more than minimum wage, but I've taken it."

"You must be relieved."

"Yeah, save up for a year and a bit and then go backpacking."

"Are you allowed out of the country?"

Daniel nodded. "I think once my sentence is over, I can do as I please. I think it'll do me some good. How about you?"

"Ken the manager is staying. He had us all individually in his office to tell us that. He told us the rota will be changing, which in my mind is good. It means the shifts will now work on a fairer basis, so we won't have to do the same shifts every week. I'll be able to have a life."

"You deserve it, mate. It's how it should be. I know it was on the news a while back about people getting more and more stressed 'cos of the work place ruling their lives. It contributed to pushing me over the edge."

Adam smiled. "Just think if you'd have stayed -"

"It was because of what I did Mark got removed. He'd still be there I'd imagine if this never happened."

Adam smiled nervously. "I'm thinking of asking Stacey out."

Daniel smiled broadly. "Don't think, just do. She's a pretty girl and you two would be well suited." They sat in silence for a minute, and then Daniel spoke.

"Do you know something? I spent the trial telling myself I was innocent. But now I think the jury were right. The sentence too. As much as I dislike Brian what I did was wrong. Violence is wrong. But that was all it took, a moment of madness and I almost threw my life away."

THIRTY-SIX

Daniel found himself sitting in the office where Woods worked a week later. He had made an appointment to see and thank him for what he did.

Woods came out of his office, smiled and said, "Come on in."

Daniel smiled and went in after him. Daniel sat opposite Woods.

"How does it feel to be walking free?" Woods asked.

"It's great. I don't worry about the suspended sentence hanging over my head either. I won't do anything else stupid. The lot I hang about with will see to it."

"With all their convictions and that?"

"Yeah, but they're right types who don't want to see me repeat their mistakes. I got a job you know?"

"Oh yeah, what as?"

"Just a factory hand in a packing factory, nothing glamorous."

"It's a start though."

"Yeah, and once my sentence is over, I think I'll go see some of the world. You know? Backpacking and that."

"I wish some days I'd done it. But I was determined to do well in my career. I don't regret it. I've got a good life. But there are always some things you wish you'd done."

"I don't know what I'll do after that, but the future is blank, and who knows what will happen."

Woods nodded at him. "How are people to you?"

"Hostile."

"It will blow over. They're just bored and have nothing better to do. I know your type, you'd probably consider it wrong to do them for harassment."

"It would just be pointless."

They sat in silence for a minute. Woods then said, "I think we've said all we have to say to each other."

"I haven't. I came here to thank you. I'd probably be in prison if it weren't for you."

"Just doing my job. And having fun upsetting Hague." Woods grinned.

Daniel laughed. "Call it what you like mate. But you did well. As you said, no Hollywood endings, but in a small way, I've had a happy ending in that I'm free. I can do what I please."

THIRTY-SEVEN

That evening, Daniel sat on a bench in Southlands Road, the same place that he had surrendered to the police all that time ago. He sat thinking of his life now. Working again, he had a proper income once he started. There was still a bit of money saved which he would save in his account for the next year or so. He felt good though. His life was badly affected, but nothing that could not be fixed.

His problems would always be there. He still had to live with his past and his special needs, but he could cope as long as he avoided losing his temper again. For now though he had a nine to five local weekday job. His mental health was priority. He would recover. He still had good friends and a family. Daniel watched a young couple go past with a little boy and girl. The boy looked at him and waved, Daniel smiled back. It was a nice evening.

END

www.eleusinianpress.co.uk

BV - #0010 - 100620 - C0 - 229/152/10 - PB - 9781909494121